THE 26TH OF NOVEMBER

A Pride and Prejudice Comedy of Farcical Proportions

By Elizabeth Adams

Copyright © 2018 by Elizabeth Adams
All rights reserved.

Dedication

*For anyone who has ever had a day they wished
they could do over. This one's for you.*

*And for my youngest daughter, who was promised
a puppy when I finished this book.*

Acknowledgements

Huge thanks to my editor, Lori Timberlake, who encouraged me from day one, listened to all my crazy ideas, and then fixed all my mistakes. My cover designer, Caitlin Daschner at Chromantic Studio, is nothing short of divine. She is helpful, kind, and a calming influence when the muse is taking me on a roller coaster ride.

My cold reader, Jami, is quickly becoming a friend, and I thank her for her solid feedback and encouragement throughout this crazy process we call writing a book. Rita at *From Pemberley to Milton* was so generous with her time and feedback, and Claudine from *Just Jane 1813* has been an absolute wonder. Her tireless efforts on behalf of writers leave me speechless and incredibly grateful.

My husband has been a rock and a huge support—listening to ideas, giving me space to write, and making sure I didn't get too lost in the project. I think we might be getting the hang of this whole creative couple thing.

Chapter 1

A Ball, a Proposal & a Letter

26th of November, Netherfield

The ball was a disaster. Elizabeth could not be more embarrassed if her family began dancing on the tabletops. Her mother was loudly proclaiming Jane's eminent engagement to Mr. Bingley, the host, and she spoke of her second daughter's betrothal to Mr. Collins, the heir to Longbourn, as if it were a completed thing. Lady Lucas was listening politely, but even that venerable gossip looked like she would happily shove a piece of bread in her neighbor's mouth if given the opportunity.

Mary had played and sung spectacularly badly and then been publicly humiliated by their father. He, of course, would stop Mary from playing in company, but would do nothing to curb her mother's tongue or stop her youngest sisters from cavorting loudly through the house, being chased by officers and drinking too much punch. Elizabeth could hear Lydia's raucous laughter from the next room, and she silently prayed the party would be rendered temporarily deaf, or better yet, her sister permanently mute.

The revulsion on the faces of Miss Bingley and Mrs. Hurst was impossible to miss, and while she would publicly defend her family, she couldn't blame the ladies' feelings. She herself was disgusted with her relations' behavior, and she had had a lifetime to become inured to it.

Mr. Darcy looked coldly at them all, staring down his aristocratic nose at the commoners of Hertfordshire. If it wasn't bad enough that he had watched her dance with the horrid Mr. Collins (and likely laughed to himself the entire time), she had been shocked into accepting a dance with him. He had gone through the steps well enough, and he had certainly been an improvement on Mr. Collins (though that was not difficult to accomplish), but they had quarreled over Mr. Wickham, and Sir William had stopped them in the middle and made an embarrassing speech about Jane and Bingley. Why had he walked through the middle of the dance anyway? Mr. Darcy's stern look toward his friend and her sister was impossible to miss. Would Mr. Darcy encourage Mr. Bingley away from Jane?

She told herself it didn't matter. Mr. Bingley was his own man, and he was clearly in love with her sister.

It was to Elizabeth's great relief that the ball ended and she found herself climbing wearily into her family's carriage. She looked out the window and ignored her mother and sisters' voices, wanting nothing more than quiet and her bed.

The next day she hoped for peace, a little solitude, and a good chat with Jane and Charlotte Lucas. Alas, it was not to be. Mr. Collins cornered her to propose and her mother insisted she hear him. It was awful and embarrassing, and she sincerely hoped she would never see him again, though she knew it to be unlikely. Her mother insisted she marry him, Elizabeth insisted she would not, and Mrs. Bennet had been angrier at her least favorite daughter than her children had ever seen her. Mary was silent, Jane squeezed her hand in support, and Lydia laughed at her, making more than one rude comment about marriage to such a man.

Thankfully, her father had supported her, even in the face of her mother's temper, and Mr. Collins had left the house for the safety of Lucas Lodge. If only her mother would keep her word about not speaking to Elizabeth ever again, she would be happy.

She lay down that night wondering what new humiliations tomorrow would bring, as the last two days had surpassed even her most horrified imaginings.

Thursday morning was bright and clear, and Elizabeth was happy to see that she'd slept until nine, even after tossing and turning for several hours. She rose hopeful that this day would be uneventful. She dressed and fixed her hair simply, then headed outside for a fortifying walk. After an hour of tramping through Longbourn's fields, she felt renewed and ready to face her mother's lamentations on her refusal to marry Mr. Collins. She stopped outside the kitchen to remove her muddy boots and asked Sarah to bring her another pair. As she was lacing them, the maid asked her if she had heard the news.

"What news?" asked Elizabeth.

"Netherfield is being closed up, Miss. I had it from my cousin Molly what works as a maid there. She was terrible upset at not having the wages through the winter. She asked if I knows of any positions in the area. I told her I'd keep my ears open."

She looked at Elizabeth expectantly.

"Of course, I will tell you if I hear of anything. My Aunt Phillips may know of a position." Sarah nodded in thanks and Elizabeth stood and straightened her gown. "The entire party left? Not just Mr. Bingley?"

"No, Miss. Molly says Mr. Bingley left yesterday as he'd planned, but then last night Miss Bingley ordered the carriage and told the housekeeper to close down the house. Said they wouldn't be back no time this winter. Molly says they left first thing this mornin', even the gentlemen."

Elizabeth looked thoughtful at this. "Mr. and Mrs. Hurst left as well?"

"Yes, Miss."

"And Mr. Darcy?"

"Yes, Miss. They've given the staff notice and Mrs. Nicholls was seein' to the drapin' of the furniture when Molly delivered a note for Mrs. Hill and told me all about it."

Elizabeth pursed her lips and wondered what this meant. Mr. Bingley would return, surely?

That afternoon, after an unsatisfactory visit to Meryton and a meeting with the charming Mr. Wickham that further turned Elizabeth's feelings against Mr. Darcy, a letter arrived for Jane from Caroline Bingley. It confirmed everything Molly had told her and furthermore dashed all of Jane's hopes as it espoused a desire to see Mr. Bingley wed to Georgiana Darcy and stated Caroline's doubts that her brother would return to the area any time soon.

Jane was devastated and felt certain that she had imagined Mr. Bingley's affections and that Caroline had kindly tried to put her on her guard. Elizabeth was less convinced and assured Jane that Mr. Bingley loved her and would return for her, but the nagging doubt in her mind would not be quiet. Her family had made a spectacle of themselves at the ball, and if she was being honest with herself, she was not surprised that the Superior Sisters thought their brother could do better. There was no one as kind or lovely as Jane herself, but Bingley was an affable, attractive man with a fortune and an easy disposition. He would likely have little trouble securing a match with a better dowered lady with fine connections.

It was no matter. She would not share her concerns with her sister. Mr. Bingley loved Jane, of that she was certain. It was only his spiteful sisters and the arrogant Mr. Darcy who were trying to convince him otherwise.

She would keep the faith—Mr. Bingley must return. But as she lay in her bed that night, she couldn't help but wish that her family had been a little less objectionable, at least in public.

Chapter 2

A Strange Dream

Elizabeth awoke to the unwelcome sound of her mother screeching. Servants were being ordered about and she was scolding her girls to get out of bed and examine their gowns for tears or loose seams. Elizabeth pressed a pillow over her head at the mention of shoe roses.

The door flew open and Mrs. Bennet burst into the room.

"Get out of bed, Miss Lizzy. You have to look your best today and Sarah will need extra time for all that hair."

She bustled out as quickly as she had come in and Elizabeth looked at her in wonder. She could have sworn her mother had said something similar to her on the morning of the Netherfield Ball, but that wasn't so unusual. Her mother had a limited repertoire of conversation.

Elizabeth dressed and went down to breakfast, searching for Jane who had uncharacteristically beaten her out of bed this morning.

"What is all the fuss about?" she asked her sister when she found her in the parlor.

Jane looked at her in confusion and said, "The ball at Netherfield, of course. What else would it be?"

Elizabeth looked at her sister in silence for more than a minute.

"Are you well, Lizzy?" asked Jane.

Elizabeth shook her head and said, "It is the strangest thing. I think I am having a dream." She pinched her arm and hissed at the pain. "Or perhaps that was the dream," she said quietly. She looked about her with a dazed expression and Jane drew close to her.

"Sister, do not let Mama see you behaving like this. She is already anxious for the ball. Perhaps you should take a short stroll in the gardens. That always refreshes you," said Jane in a low voice.

Elizabeth agreed and took herself to the garden and wandered aimlessly through the rows of late blooming dahlias and goldenrod. It was so very strange. It had all felt so real!

She sighed in relief that Bingley was still at Netherfield and Jane's heart was unbroken. All would be well. It was just a dream.

Mr. Collins showed his first bit of sense and left the ladies to their preparations. He had been following Elizabeth like a puppy and she was glad of a respite from his attentions. She dressed with care and spent an hour on her hair. She had hopes that Mr. Wickham would be there and he would ask for a dance. He had hinted as much when she last saw him. He had been absent from the ball in her dream, but she would not let that deter her hopes.

She had not been at the ball above a quarter hour when she realized Mr. Wickham was not there. She was told he had not come because of Darcy, and the hope of avoiding a public conflict. The similarity to her dream confused her, but she nodded and found her friends. Her first set was with Mr. Collins, and it was awful. He stepped on her foot more than once, apologized instead of attended, and made a general fool of himself and her as his partner.

Mr. Darcy stalked around the edge of the ballroom, his eyes sometimes on her, and she felt herself flush that such an arrogant man should see her dancing with a buffoon. Finally, the dance was over and Elizabeth felt nothing but relief as she hurried away from Mr. Collins.

She was talking to Charlotte when she was approached, quite suddenly, by Mr. Darcy. He asked her to dance the next and she accepted, too flustered to think of a suitable excuse to avoid his company.

By the time her dance with Mr. Darcy began, she was beginning to wonder if she had a gift of premonition. So far, the evening had progressed nearly exactly as it had in her dream, the only differences being her own words and reactions. Wishing to test her theory, she made a remark about the dance.

He was silent, as she thought he would be.

"It is your turn to say something now, Mr. Darcy. I talked about the dance, now you ought to make some remark about the size of the room, or the number of couples."

He smiled and said, "Whatever you wish me to say shall be said."

A nervous feeling crept over the edges of her mind. "Very well, that reply will do for the present," she said, with less gaiety than she might have. "Perhaps by and by I might observe that private balls are pleasanter than public ones. But now we may be silent."

She said the lines as if reading from a script, her cheeks beginning to pink and her eyes not meeting his.

"Do you talk by rule then, when you are dancing?" he asked.

She swallowed and smiled weakly, glad the dance was taking them away from each other for a moment. Was she a prophetess? She vaguely recalled hearing of prophets when her grandmother would read the Bible to them, but that had been years ago. Perhaps Mary would know.

She returned to Mr. Darcy and endeavored to keep her composure. She knew what would be said. She would call him taciturn, he would be evasive, she would question him about his tendency to be resentful and they would quarrel about Wickham. He would ask her not to sketch his character at that time and she would say she would have no other opportunity. He would grudgingly acquiesce, and they would dance in silence.

Her heart beating rapidly, Elizabeth turned about Mr. Darcy, then joined the ladies in a circle. Her mind was spinning faster than the dance. How had this happened?

She said nothing else, and Mr. Darcy looked at her oddly more than once, but she had no desire to further confirm her fears. When she saw Sir William crossing the floor, she turned in a wrong direction and he passed them while she apologized to the lady she had run into. Darcy looked at her quizzically again, but she ignored him and went through the remainder of the dance mechanically. Darcy led her to her mother when the dance was over, thanked her, bowed correctly, and left. She vaguely noted that if the events in her dream truly were premonitions or prophesies, she would never see him again, for he would leave in two days' time.

The remainder of the evening only further disturbed Elizabeth. Her father interrupted Mary on the pianoforte—again—and ignored her younger sisters' wild behavior. Lydia and Kitty drank too much, spoke too loudly, and flirted with everything in a red coat. Her mother spoke so volubly at dinner that Elizabeth wished she could crawl under the table as she had done when she was four years old. She was too worried about her own predicament to notice the glares aimed at her family by Mr. Darcy and the Superior Sisters, but she knew they were there nonetheless.

As she finally climbed into bed that night, fully aware that she had just experienced the same day twice and wondering if she had a mystical gift for foresight—like a gypsy—she said a fervent prayer that Mr. Collins would not propose to her tomorrow and she would return to her usual ungifted self.

~

She was to be disappointed. The next day began with her mother screeching and telling her to wake up, for her hair would take additional time to arrange. Somehow, against all reason and rationality, it was Tuesday, the 26th of November. Again.

Elizabeth trudged to the breakfast table in a sour mood, and then settled into her father's library with the Bible to read about prophets. She read everything she could think of that might explain premonitions, prophesies, even witchcraft. None of it explained her experience or was in the least bit helpful.

Her father asked her what she was about, and she said she was merely curious about something. After watching him do nothing to curb her sisters' behavior at the same ball twice, she was not feeling particularly forthcoming. He went back to his book as she knew he would and ignored her for the remainder of the day. She supposed she should be grateful he had not asked her to leave, though she expected he had likely forgotten her presence some hours ago.

She was late to begin preparing for the ball and her hair was put up simply. Jane had kindly attached her shoe roses for her and helped her latch her necklace moments before they rushed out the door.

The evening progressed as she knew it would, Elizabeth left the ball more discouraged than ever, and she once more went to bed fervently praying this strangeness would end.

Chapter 3

In Which Elizabeth Tells Many Falsehoods

The oddity that had become Elizabeth's life continued for three more days before she decided to do something about it. She would not normally be so slow to act, but she had been so very befuddled, so utterly flummoxed, that she could not think what she *could* do, nor what she should.

She began to think of her dilemma as a puzzle. Every puzzle had an answer, an ending of some sort. Was there an answer to the question of why she was repeating the same day over and over? She did not know if there was one, but if there was the slightest chance that there was a method to all this madness, she would find it out.

She thought of the first ball. It had been an enjoyable evening until it had not. Jane had had a lovely time, but Elizabeth had gone from one humiliation to the next. However, none of this was terribly unexpected. The first ball had been followed by two days into the future, as she now began to think of it (and desperately long for it).

She analyzed those days, thinking the answer may lie there since she had only experienced them once. Of course, it was just as likely that the answer was not in those two days and that was why she did not repeat them, but she made a list of everything that had happened regardless.

It had been an eventful time. Mr. Bingley left for what was supposed to be a short trip to London. Mr. Collins presented Elizabeth with an unwanted proposal, and the Netherfield party left Hertfordshire for an indefinite period of time. The most innocuous occurrence was Mr. Bingley's leaving. It had been planned for some time, and she supposed he had not gone before the ball because he was needed for preparations or perhaps because of the week of rain they had experienced.

Yet, she couldn't help thinking that had he not left, his party would not have followed him. She couldn't forget Jane's face when she read Miss Bingley's letter saying they had closed the house and were eagerly anticipating spending the winter in company with Miss Darcy. Elizabeth felt certain Caroline was lying, but would Mr. Bingley's regard be strong enough to draw him back to Hertfordshire? He had an easy temperament and was often swayed by his friends' inclinations. He'd admitted as much himself.

Was it in her power to make him stay? Would that accomplish anything of significance, or only delay his departure? If he had business in Town, he would have to go eventually.

Regardless, she thought it was as good a possibility as anything. She would do everything she could to make Mr. Bingley stay at Netherfield.

~

Elizabeth danced the first with Mr. Collins, as she had promised, but now she was familiar with his mistakes and was able to spare her feet from his clumsiness. The second was promised to an officer, but the third was free. She had previously spent this dance speaking with Charlotte Lucas, but this time she purposely sought out Mr. Bingley. He had opened with Jane, danced the second with his sister, and had previously danced the third with one of the Miss Longs. Before he could reach those fair ladies, Elizabeth intercepted him and began telling him what a lovely party it was and how he had done the beautiful house justice. He was pleased with her compliments and responded warmly, then asked her to dance the next when the couples began lining up.

They talked of general things for a few minutes before she began her attack.

"My mother has tasked me with giving you a dinner invitation," she said.

"That is very kind of her. I leave for Town tomorrow, but when I return, I shall be glad to accept," he replied with good humor.

"When do you return?"

"I hope to complete my business in a few days, but mayhap it will require a week."

She nodded thoughtfully. "Shall I tell my mother you will come Thursday next? That will give you plenty of time to return." She smiled sweetly and turned around him as the dance called for.

He thought for a moment, then smiled brightly. "Yes, I think that shall do splendidly! I shall ask my sisters if they are available."

Elizabeth nodded in response and wondered what else she could do. Was an accepted invitation enough to bring him back? Surely not. If his heart was not enough, dinner certainly wouldn't be.

"I was wondering if you would consent to help me with something when you return," she said.

He looked surprised. "Of course, Miss Elizabeth. What do you require?"

She thought frantically and finally said, "I would like to sponsor a contest with the estate children. Winter can be a difficult time, as you know, and I had thought it would be nice to give them something to look forward to, and some provisions to assist their families. I had thought the two estates could do it together, since the tenant families know one another and many are friends."

"That sounds like a marvelous idea! What kind of contest did you have in mind?"

At a loss for a plausible idea, she said, "That is what I was hoping you could help me with. I had thought of some sport, but the weather is too cold for that. For indoor pursuits, we could do sewing for the girls, but I know not what would be suitable for the boys. I have no brothers, so I thought you might have a suggestion."

A sewing contest? Really, Lizzy. You can do better than that!

She smiled and he thought for a moment.

"Do you know if the children play checkers?"

"Checkers? That is a wonderful idea!" She knew she was overly enthusiastic, but she simply must give him a reason to stay!

"You could run it as a tournament, as they do for chess. Have you already chosen a prize? I would like to contribute, of course."

She nodded. "That is very kind of you, Mr. Bingley. I had thought half a crown each for one girl and one boy."

He nodded thoughtfully. "It is a fine idea. I should like to assist you. We may discuss the details at dinner next week," he said, full of enthusiasm.

She agreed and the dance ended. He led her off the floor and she chastised herself for not accomplishing her goal. She had intended to stop him from leaving altogether, not to encourage him to come back! She frowned and told herself it didn't matter, what was done was done. Perhaps knowing he had someone expecting him and relying upon his assistance would create a greater urgency to return. If he told his sisters about it, they may not follow him to Town.

Elizabeth stopped walking and stared ahead of her blankly, wondering at her own stupidity. Of course Mr. Bingley would return on his own, he had already said he would and he had every reason to come back. The only thing that would keep him in London was his sisters, and perhaps Mr. Darcy. She should have directed her efforts at convincing *them* to stay in Hertfordshire, not Mr. Bingley! Stupid girl!

Elizabeth knew that no number of commitments would keep Caroline Bingley anywhere she did not want to be. She would simply write a note and give her excuses, then do exactly what she pleased. She imagined Mr. Darcy was the same. Mrs. Hurst might be more easily worked on, but then she likely would not stand up to her more forceful sister.

What to do, what to do?

Mr. Darcy was advancing toward her, and knowing she had danced the fourth set with him at every ball she had attended thus far, she agreed graciously and was silent for the first several minutes, furiously thinking of a way to keep this man in Meryton.

"Will you be staying long in the country, Mr. Darcy?" she asked.

"I will return to Town for the festive season to collect my sister."

"Will you remain in Town until the Season, or will you travel to Derbyshire?"

He looked at her quizzically for a moment, then answered, "If the roads are good, we will travel to Derbyshire. I will return to Town in April."

She nodded in response and couldn't feel irritated by his strange looks. She had never really asked him about himself or his plans before. He must find it odd.

"Will you accompany Mr. Bingley to Town tomorrow?"

"I had not planned to, no."

He looked at her curiously again and she found herself forming a desperate resolution. Caroline held sway over her brother, and she wanted nothing more than to be Mrs. Darcy. She would not leave if Darcy stayed, and Mr. Bingley would surely return if his guests were still in residence. But how to get him to stay? He likely wouldn't accept a dinner invitation or feel obligated by one if he did. Elizabeth was certainly not attractive enough to him to achieve anything by flirting, and she wouldn't know how to go about enticing a man to remain in the area while not actually encouraging him romantically—as if such arts would work on Mr. Darcy.

"My father mentioned that he hasn't had much chance to converse with you," she said when the dance brought them together again.

"No, we have not spoken much," he answered, his face blank.

"He has been lamenting of late the lack of good chess partners in the area. His favorite partner has recently moved to his son in Stoke. Do you play?"

"Yes, I do."

She smiled brightly. "Would you play a game with my father? I should not make plans for him, but I know he has been long desiring a game since his friend moved away, and it would cheer him considerably to play with an able opponent."

She smiled again and they separated in the dance. Elizabeth was beginning to fear for her sanity. She had lost count of how many falsehoods she had uttered in the last hour and she was surprised at the ridiculous words spewing from her mouth.

"I should like a game with your father," he said when they were joined again by the dance.

"Splendid!" she cried. "Will Friday suit?"

"Yes, I shall plan on it," he said solemnly.

She granted him yet another smile and they completed the dance in silence.

The ball continued as it always did, and she could only hope her paltry efforts had made some kind of difference.

~

The next morning, she awoke praying it was Wednesday, the day after the ball, and not Tuesday, the day of the ball. Her mother shrieking in the hall was proof that she had failed in her plan to keep the Netherfield party in Hertfordshire. If that was indeed the purpose of this enterprise.

She would have to be more convincing tonight.

Elizabeth entered the ball with one goal: convince Caroline

Bingley to stay in Hertfordshire. She was kind to the lady, complimented her on the arrangements, and told her how lovely her skin looked and that it must be the effect of all the country air. Caroline thanked her and looked thoughtful for a moment.

At supper, Elizabeth—through sheer force of personality—cajoled Mr. Darcy into sitting next to Caroline. Elizabeth felt like an animal keeper, feeding a snake a particularly plump mouse, but if Caroline was the key to her escaping this nightmare, Elizabeth would give her whatever she wanted.

Caroline seemed pleased at Elizabeth's delivery and Elizabeth risked giving the lady a sly wink as she sat on the opposite side of Mr. Darcy. Miss Bingley looked surprised, but quickly recovered. Both ladies knew that Caroline's best chances of winning Mr. Darcy were at Netherfield, where they shared a residence. If they both returned to London, Caroline would go to her sister's house and Mr. Darcy would go to his. She would have considerably less access to him. It was clearly in her favor to remain in the country.

Every time Mr. Darcy's attention turned to Elizabeth, she somehow redirected it to Caroline. She was at her charming best, surprising herself at how affable she could be to two people she heartily disliked and was further shocked by receiving Mr. Darcy's affability in return. Caroline was very pleasant as well, and she and Elizabeth worked in concert to entertain the gentleman. All three seemed slightly disturbed by their camaraderie.

Mr. Darcy and Miss Bingley were so consumed by Elizabeth's attentions that they barely noticed Mary's discordant playing or her father's rude dismissal. When Lydia ran past them shrieking, they looked up for a moment, but were then drawn back into their own conversation.

Elizabeth wondered why she hadn't thought of it before. Mr. Darcy and Miss Bingley were clearly the ones in control of this company, Miss Bingley especially. Trying to convince Mr. Bingley of anything had been a waste of valuable time. These two were the decision makers.

It was a subtle plan, and one she was by no means sure of, but she thought it had as good a chance as any.

~

She was wrong. The next day was Tuesday. She met it with a groan and began to formulate her plan. Now realizing that Caroline was her true quarry, she set to work thinking of a suitable way to make the lady remain in the country.

"Have you had a letter from Town lately, Miss Bingley?" Elizabeth asked at the ball. She had remembered to be kind and flattering first, to soften the lady up, and had repeated her comment about her skin looking brighter from the clean country air.

"No, Miss Eliza. My friends are in the country for the winter," she said, as if it was a ridiculous question.

"Oh, well then you will not have heard news of the outbreak."

"Outbreak?" asked Caroline.

"Yes. I've had a letter from my aunt just today." She would have to add that to her growing list of falsehoods. "Typhoid fever is spreading through the city like wildfire," she said dramatically.

Caroline's eyes widened, and Elizabeth successfully hid her smile.

"Is it very widespread?" asked Miss Bingley. She looked truly frightened and Elizabeth felt a moment of guilt, but she had come too far to stop now.

"I'm afraid it is. My aunt and uncle usually come to Longbourn for the festive season without the children, but they will bring them this year to keep them safe, and they are talking of arriving earlier than usual, perhaps as early as next week."

Caroline's eyes widened. "It is as bad as that, then?"

"It is best in these situations to be careful, I believe. I haven't mentioned it to my mother or sisters. I didn't want to ruin their evening with worrying over our friends in Town. You won't mention it to them, will you?"

"Of course not, Miss Eliza. I am more than capable of keeping a confidence," replied Miss Bingley.

"Your brother mentioned he is going to Town for business tomorrow. Please do tell him to take care. I would hate for him to become ill," Elizabeth said sincerely.

"Yes, I will mention it, of course. Thank you for the information, Eliza."

Elizabeth nodded and left the lady to her ruminations, thinking this had been a much better method than the previous ones she had employed.

~

Alas, though it had been a very good idea (she couldn't help admitting such to herself), it did not work. Tuesday rose again the next day and Elizabeth found herself once again preparing for a ball.

Feeling desperate, she went to the stables and started a conversation with Old John. He had been the coachman and stablemaster at Longbourn for as long as she could remember. When she was a small child, she would sit on a hay bale and watch him at his work, fascinated by the strange equipment and the majestic animals.

"Good day," she said when she entered the stable.

Old John was surprised to see her, but also quite pleased, and their conversation progressed amiably.

"I wonder if you would explain something to me," she said eventually.

"Of course, Miss Lizzy. What can I help ye with?"

"I read in a book recently how a carriage broke down, and the way the author described it made little sense to me. Would you mind showing me how it can be done?"

He nodded and took her to the carriage, which had been cleaned and shined in preparation for the ball. He showed her all the various parts, and what was responsible for which action. When she told him she had read of carriages losing wheels and breaking axles, and asked how such a thing could come about, he showed her how losing a wheel could be as simple as a bad bolt and easily remedied. An axle was a larger problem and could take a few days to fix.

"It must be a terrible accident to cause an axle to break," she said with wide eyes.

"Ye'd be surprised," he replied. He went on to explain how the wrong distribution of weight or an uneven surface could put strain on the axle and its accompanying parts.

She listened with rapt attention and thanked him for taking the time to talk to her. He bowed gallantly and she gave him a sweet smile before returning to the house. She slipped into Kitty's room and found an old play dress, one that could pass for a servants' Sunday wear, and stuffed it into a small bag. Then she told her mother she would take a nap to be fresh for the ball. Her mother agreed that she needed all the help with her looks she could get and shooed her to her room. Elizabeth put pillows under her blanket so it would appear she was buried beneath the covers and snuck out the servants' door. Once she gained the ground floor, she crept out one of the back doors and made her way to the shed. She gathered the tools she needed, then struck out towards Netherfield.

Once she was a good distance from Longbourn, she ducked behind a large tree and changed her dress for the one she had pilfered from her sister. She put on an old bonnet that had seen better days and pulled it low so her hair was completely covered. She contemplated smudging dirt on her face, but there were few dirty housemaids or tenants that near to the house.

She was so anxious over her plan that she arrived at Netherfield in very good time. She watched the stables carefully from her hiding place behind a dense thicket at the edge of the forest. She knew not how many men were employed there nor where they were located.

Luck was on her side. A maid exited the kitchen door and was soon at the stables, announcing the midday meal was ready if they cared to partake. Three men filed out of the stables and followed her up to the house. Elizabeth was about to sneak out from her hiding place when she heard steps and two more men rushed out, dressed differently than the others. Hoping that was everyone, she crept slowly to the stables and looked around, straining her ears for sounds of steps or voices.

All was quiet. She crept into the stables and moved quickly to the far end of the building where the carriages were housed in a connected structure. Thankfully, the large carriage doors were closed and no one would see her in the shadowy space. A horse whinnied as she passed his box and she nearly jumped at the sound of it, then placed her hand over her racing heart and continued on her path.

There were two carriages. One had what she assumed was the Darcy crest on it. It looked pretentious even in the dim light of the carriage house. Unsure which they would ride in, and knowing they could simply take the other if one was damaged, she decided to sabotage both.

She set to work on the Bingley carriage—she recognized it from Caroline's call at Longbourn. She removed the small saw she had taken from the shed and began working on the axle. She wanted to be sure a simple repair was not possible, so she sawed straight through one side, then slid over on the dirty ground to the other. There was straw on the ground, she assumed to protect the carriage from the mud all the recent rain had caused, and it cushioned her knees somewhat, but it was an awkward position crouching under a carriage.

The saw made an awful amount of noise and every minute she was sure someone would return and drag her out by her ear. She would have to admit her identity to avoid terrible punishment, and that would lead to terrible humiliation. These thoughts almost made her cease her actions, but then she remembered that tomorrow would be a fresh day, and no one would remember what had happened today if she was not successful. Comforted by that thought, she attacked the axle on the second carriage with renewed vigor and soon, both carriages were lame. She packed up her saw and was about to exit the carriage house when men's voices were heard coming into the adjacent stable.

Elizabeth held her breath and scooted to the back corner, wondering how she would escape unseen. She couldn't open the carriage house doors. They were too large to be opened unnoticed and she had never opened one, either. It was hardly something she could do quickly and under duress. Just when she was thinking she would have to hide there for hours until the men left again, she noticed a sliver of light far to her right. A door!

She crept quietly to it and saw there were several empty crates stacked in front of it. It was clearly not used often. She hoped it still opened; she examined it closely and saw it wasn't boarded up and the lock wasn't rusted through. She began moving the crates one by one, grateful they were small enough for her to lift, though her arms were burning by the third one. She was on the fourth and final crate when she heard a voice—a dangerously close voice. She set the crate down as quietly as she could as the voice moved closer and closer, and she prayed harder than she ever had that the door would open easily and quietly. She turned the key in the lock and cringed at the squeaking sound it made, but rejoiced that it turned at all. She looked over her shoulder in time to see a man's shadow thrown across the doorway; he paused to yell something back into the stables. She opened the creaking door just enough to squeeze through, then closed it swiftly behind her. It had not been silent, but it hadn't been loud either, and she hoped the man thought it was the horses and other grooms and not an intruder.

If they found the damaged axles too soon, they would have them repaired before the party left on Thursday, perhaps Friday. She would have only delayed them by a day, maybe only a few hours, and all this subterfuge and terror would have been for nothing.

Elizabeth dashed into the trees behind the stables, moving as swiftly and quietly as she could. Once she gained the cover of the forest, she ran along the familiar path as fast as her legs could take her. She was nearing Longbourn when she stopped to catch her breath. Her lungs and legs were burning, her eyes wild and her heart nearly beating out of her chest.

She had just snuck onto someone else's property and willfully damaged his carriage. She. Elizabeth Bennet! It was so very unladylike, and so very disturbing, that she could not prevent nervous laughter from escaping her throat as she tugged off the old bonnet and her sister's worn dress. She slipped back into her own gown and splashed cold water onto her face and neck from an obliging stream. It chilled her as it ran down her breastbone, but calmed her breathing and her nerves. She welcomed it with relief.

She snuck back into Longbourn and up the back stairs, unseen by everyone but Sarah, who was well familiar with her outdoor habits. The maid winked and offered to bring hot water up as soon as it was ready. Elizabeth could only thank her and collapse on the bed, her nerves utterly shattered.

Chapter 4

A New Tactic

Elizabeth's devastation at waking up to yet another Tuesday knew no bounds. She cried in her bed for nearly an hour, then uncharacteristically took Nelly out for a ride. She had a need to go further than her own feet could take her. She vaguely wondered if riding far enough away would do any good, but she had a very strong feeling it would not. By the time she returned to Longbourn, her mother was looking for her and Jane informed her that she had held her off as long as possible.

Elizabeth apologized and gave an excuse, then prepared for the ball. She thought over her situation while Sarah was brushing and pinning her hair. She had been so sure the key to ending this madness was keeping the Netherfield party in Meryton. She again reviewed the first day of the ball and the two following it, the "original days," as she had come to think of them. Time had begun repeating itself the day the Netherfield party left. Surely that was significant?

But she had done everything in her power to keep them here and none of it had worked. She had tried to delay Caroline by more than one tactic and had not been successful. Mr. Darcy had agreed to stay on through the end of the week to meet with her father, and she thought he was the kind of man who would not agree to something he did not truly want to do, but that had not worked either. She had delayed Mr. Bingley himself, secured promises to return from the same gentleman, and sabotaged the ability to leave of the entire party.

But had she truly? She realized with a sinking heart that Mr. Bingley might have chosen to go to London on horseback. And if he did, when the remaining party decided to leave, they would discover the damaged carriages, have them repaired, and be on their way. Mr.

Darcy and Mr. Hurst might even go ahead on horseback, though she would be shocked to see Mr. Hurst doing anything so active as riding.

She realized with a heavy heart that unless she somehow made lame every horse in the stable, which she did not have the slightest desire nor ability to do, she would not be able to keep the men here. And were they not the principal characters in the drama she was trapped in? Mr. Bingley was the one she most wanted to detain, and Miss Bingley would go wherever Mr. Darcy led. Perhaps keeping the Netherfield party in Hertfordshire for more than a few days was impossible. And if it was so, she was wasting her time and energy on a fruitless pursuit.

Feeling utterly hopeless, she climbed into the carriage with her family for yet another Netherfield Ball.

"Do you believe in premonitions, Mr. Darcy?" she asked as they danced together. She had grown tired of being silent and though he was an aloof man, he was intelligent and her best chance for stimulating conversation.

"In what sort of situation?" he asked, his surprise at her question evident.

"Any sort of situation!" she cried. "You either believe it to be possible or you do not. The belief does not change with the surroundings."

He looked thoughtful and stared above her, perhaps at nothing, and they were silent for several movements. Finally, he spoke. "I must say that I do, Miss Elizabeth."

She could not help the look of shock that leapt onto her countenance.

"I see I have surprised you," he said with a small smile.

"Yes, I will admit that you have. I would not have thought you the sort of man who would believe in such a thing."

He tilted his head slightly and gazed at her as they circled each other.

"Perhaps I should not be astonished," she said, unnerved by his lack of response and his unwavering gaze. "I do not know you well." She surprised herself slightly with the last statement. It was true, she supposed. She knew the sort of man he was, but she did not know him personally, as such.

"I cannot argue with that," he said with a nod. The dance brought their hands together and he spoke quietly. "I have personally experienced a sense of danger, a foreboding, if you will, and it has stood me in good stead these many years, as well as those I hold dear."

"Would you care to elaborate?" she asked curiously.

His jaw clenched and his posture stiffened, but he finally said quietly, "Once, when I was a boy, I was riding at Pemberley with my cousin. He is a few years my senior and we knew the landscape well. We had every reason to believe we were safe." The dance separated them again and he continued when they came together, his arm extended as she trailed under it. "We were riding up a hill and I signaled to him that we should veer right, away from the crest of the hill. He did not understand why I changed directions, and to be honest I could not say either. I just felt very strongly that I should go another way."

"What happened?" she asked.

"Two things, really. We rode along a stream and were of some help to a tenant child who had gotten himself too high in a tree. But when we returned to the house, we were told that an old well had caved in on the southern end of the estate. Having just come from that area, we asked where it was exactly."

"Was it on the other side of the hill you did not ride over?" she asked eagerly.

"Yes, it was. I rode out and saw it the next day. It was a deep hole and the land around it had sunk as well. It would have been directly in our path had we charged over the hill as we were planning to do."

"So you had a lucky escape," she said thoughtfully.

"Yes, we certainly did."

"And the tenant child was likely grateful for your assistance as well." She smiled and tripped about him in a circle.

"I suppose he was, though my valet was not happy that I had ruined perfectly good breeches with climbing trees."

She laughed and he blushed slightly. She imagined the fastidious Mr. Darcy rarely told such personal information to barely tolerable ladies of his acquaintance. But she couldn't bring herself to be angry with him. He had given her much to think on.

She contemplated Mr. Darcy's tale the remainder of the evening. Did she normally have such intuition herself? She had always thought herself a great judge of character, but that was hardly a premonition or anything more than observation skills. For example, she reasoned, she knew Mr. Darcy was taciturn and difficult because he refused to speak in company and called her tolerable and not handsome enough to tempt him for something as simple as a dance. And he had scared away Mr. Wickham.

She paused at that thought. She heard Mr. Wickham's voice in her head, so many days ago now, telling her it was for Darcy to avoid him if he did not want to be in company with his old friend. He was going to attend the ball and dance every dance—he was not afraid of Mr. Darcy, no matter how rich and tall he was. But Mr. Wickham had not attended, had he? She knew the ball better than anyone now, and she knew every officer was present except for Mr. Wickham. He had gone to London on business for his superiors. He had asked for the assignment. He had wanted to avoid Mr. Darcy.

How odd, she thought suddenly. The ball was well attended and in a large home. It would have been easy for Mr. Wickham to evade Mr. Darcy there had he not wanted to cause a scene or have an awkward encounter. Why say he would go when he would not?

For that matter, why was no one doing as they said they would do? Miss Bingley pretended friendship to Jane, then snuck away with her entire party without taking leave of the neighborhood. Mr. Wickham said he would not avoid Darcy, but avoid him he had. Mr. Darcy insulted her and stared at her, then asked her to dance! Mr. Bingley acted as if he loved Jane, but Elizabeth was certain that he would not return, for why would it be so important for her to keep the party from leaving if he intended to come back in a week?

Even time was not behaving as it always had! Her life had become a farce of immense proportions and she wished nothing more than to return to her usual existence.

~

The next ball, during her fourth set, the one she always danced with Mr. Darcy, she asked him again about premonitions, hoping he would tell her something he hadn't the night before.

"Once, someone close to me nearly made a very foolish mistake. Luckily, I had a feeling that I was needed. I arrived in time to stop anything irreversible from happening."

"That is very cryptic of you, Mr. Darcy," she teased, wanting to lighten the suddenly heavy atmosphere.

He said nothing else and they completed the dance in near silence.

~

Elizabeth awoke to Tuesday again, having run out of ideas for the moment. She was beginning to become inured to it and decided to enjoy herself today—she could make a new plan tomorrow—or today again, as it were. She went for a stroll in the dormant gardens, stopping to admire a late-blooming dahlia that was holding out desperately against the chill in the air. She took her father tea in his bookroom and went to the music room to practice the pianoforte. She generally only practiced an hour or two a week, but with all her time lately spent preparing for the ball, she found that she missed the instrument. She remained there for nearly two hours until her mother insisted she begin her preparations.

"Good evening, Mr. Darcy," she said cheerfully when he approached her at Netherfield.

Charlotte looked at her in surprise and Mr. Darcy seemed somewhat taken aback himself. Elizabeth continued to smile and await his request. She had danced with him several times now, and he was much preferable to her cousin and most of the officers, even if his conversation was somewhat lacking—though she could admit he had been slightly more interesting lately. And he was clean and smelled nice, which could not be said of all the gentlemen present.

She smiled over her shoulder to Charlotte as he led her to the floor and stifled a laugh at her friend's expression. The set had two dances; the first was a lively, invigorating piece and the second was more sedate and suited to conversation. Darcy was an excellent partner—always where he was supposed to be, in perfect time to the music, never leering down her gown. She went through the dance in good cheer and couldn't keep the smile from her face at the sheer absurdity of it. That Mr. Darcy should be her preferred partner! And all because he had a wonderful sense of rhythm and kept his eyes above her neck. It really was impossible not to smile. He seemed affected by her frivolity and smiled at her in return, his eyes shining with a strange light.

They made a few comments in passing in the first dance, and just before it ended, Elizabeth asked him if he believed in premonitions, or intuition.

"Do you, Miss Bennet?"

Oh, this was new!

She quirked a brow. "As a matter of fact, Mr. Darcy, I do."

He nodded his deference and she thought quickly on how to prove her assertion. "Sir William is headed this way. I predict he will cross the middle of the floor, stop us in the dance, and comment on how much he enjoys seeing us partake in the activity."

"I do not know how intuitive such a prediction is, Miss Bennet," replied Darcy. "That sounds very much like something Sir William would say. Mayhap you are only utilizing your cleverness and not any higher powers."

She smiled and shook her head. "I do not know what I am more astonished by: that you think me clever, or that we are having such a pleasant conversation without arguing."

He studied her for a moment, then said, "You are the cleverest woman of my acquaintance, Miss Bennet."

She blushed to the roots of her hair and could do nothing but stare dumbly at him.

Sir William then stopped and spoke almost exactly as she had predicted. Recovering from what she thought might be the greatest compliment anyone had ever given her, she drew her attention to the conversation. She gave Darcy pointed looks throughout and his expression remained neutral, though she thought she saw humor in his eyes. She jumped in before Sir William could mention Jane or Mr. Bingley—every time her neighbor had mentioned them before, Darcy's expression had darkened, and she had no desire to end such a pleasant dance with animosity.

When Sir William left, she gave Darcy a smug expression and he looked at her and shook his head. She was sure he would have rolled his eyes if such behavior wasn't beneath him.

~

Elizabeth awoke less cheerful the next day, knowing she had no great plan to return herself to normalcy. She did think about it as she was playing the instrument and checking her mulberry wine in the stillroom. Alas, the stillroom was bereft of inspiration and she returned to the house in depressed spirits.

She decided to try a new hairstyle and caught the maid before she could work on any of her sisters. She was likely successful because the ball was still five hours away. Her hair had always held a style remarkably long, and she wasn't doing anything so vigorous it would ruin it before the ball.

She tried to look on her situation with equanimity. If she was doomed to replay the same day over and over, there were worse days than a ball surrounded by friends. If only Lydia would be less mortifying. And her mother less voluble. And Mary less determined to exhibit her poor musical skills.

Elizabeth went to her sister's room, an idea suddenly springing to her mind.

"Mary, are you ready for the evening?" she asked.

Her sister looked surprised to see her there and Elizabeth tried to put her at ease. Eventually she asked Mary if she planned to play. Mary said she did and before she could name the piece she had chosen—and played badly every night of the ball—Elizabeth leapt in.

"I wish you would play this one. You play it so well, and it has always been a favorite of mine. It would give me great joy to hear you play it tonight." She passed the sheet music to Mary.

Mary didn't quite know what to say and thanked her sister. Elizabeth could only hope she had achieved at least one of her goals and set out to speak to her father about Kitty and Lydia.

"Do you really think they are prepared for such a ball?" she asked Mr. Bennet from her perch on the worn chair in front of his desk.

"There will be no peace in this house if they do not go," he said wearily.

"Yes, but we will not be here to hear their lamentations," she said.

He smiled. "Your logic is sound, but they will complain for weeks and so will your mother, and I do not wish to hear it. It is only a neighborhood ball."

Elizabeth felt herself growing frustrated and losing hold of her earlier sanguinity. "Papa, if you do not take the trouble to check them, they will become the most determined flirts to ever make themselves or their family ridiculous. At least keep Lydia home! She is but fifteen!"

She could see by his countenance that he would not yield, but she had one further thing to add.

"We must think of Jane. She cares deeply for Mr. Bingley, and I believe he cares for her, as does anyone who has ever seen them together. But what prudent man would wish to marry into a foolish family when there is a very high likelihood that those fools will one day call his home their own?"

Mr. Bennet understood the implied insult—he had not prepared his daughters well for his death, and he had not raised them to be proper ladies either.

"Forgive me, Father, but I must speak plainly. Jane's happiness may depend on it. Mr. Bingley is not a forceful man and he has the responsibility of his sister. She does not want him to marry Jane, that much is clear."

He raised his brows at this. "What makes you say that? And why should Mr. Bingley listen to his sister?"

"Miss Bingley's disdain is obvious, especially when she is not in larger company, and her fate is tied to her brother's, as they both know. He will consider her in whatever decision he makes. We do not have large dowries or grand connections. Must the family make it more difficult for Jane than it is already? Does she not have enough obstacles to overcome with no resources but her beauty and her kindness?"

Mr. Bennet seemed taken aback, and Elizabeth knew she had said far more than her father had ever thought to hear from a daughter, or from anyone. To be called to the carpet by one's own child! Elizabeth felt shame run through her, but she could not forget Jane's face when Miss Bingley's letter arrived informing them of the party's departure and unlikely return. For her sister, she would do what was required.

"Wherever you or Jane are known you will be valued. And any callow youth that will be run off by a little silliness is not worth the trouble of worrying over," said Mr. Bennet, interpreting her upset as needless worry over her own prospects.

"But it is not just a little silliness! It is humiliation, pure and distilled and displayed for public consumption."

Elizabeth felt tears of frustration pricking at her eyes. He would not see! Nothing she said would make him see.

"Forgive me, Father," she whispered and rushed from the room.

She cried in her bed for some time until she gave herself a headache. Deciding she did not care either way, she told the maid she would not go the ball as she was ill. She took a sleeping powder and was nearly asleep when her mother bustled in. Seeing Elizabeth's red-rimmed eyes, pink nose, and puffy cheeks, she decided it was better if she stayed home than ruin the family's collective looks. Elizabeth could only nod weakly and curl under her blanket. She didn't even hear her father when he stepped into her room in the early hours of the morning after the ball and knelt by the bed, saying, "You are right, Lizzy. I shall try to do better."

Little did he know he would not get the chance.

Chapter 5

A Fortunate Mishap

If the conversation with her father had taught her anything, it was that people are unalterable. They are who they are and they will behave as themselves, no matter how much we might wish them to do otherwise.

With that thought in mind, Elizabeth rushed up the stairs after breaking her fast just as Lydia was sleepily coming down. She ran headlong into her sister and Lydia stumbled and fell the last four steps, landing in a heap at the bottom.

"Lizzy! You ran into me!" cried Lydia loudly.

"I am so sorry, Lyddie. Let me help you up."

Elizabeth squatted near her sister and wrapped an arm around her, helping her to stand. Lydia winced as she put weight on her foot and leaned heavily on Elizabeth.

"Oh, no!" cried Lydia.

Her wails brought the household running and soon they had helped her to a sofa in the drawing room.

"Oh, my poor child! What happened? How could you do such a thing? And on the day of the ball! What are we to do!" shrieked Mrs. Bennet.

Jane was attempting to soothe both her mother and her youngest sister, while Elizabeth placed a cushion under Lydia's ankle. Lydia continued to whine about the pain, and how clumsy Elizabeth was, and how very unfair this entire day was turning out, even though it was only mid-morning.

Mrs. Bennet eventually stopped wailing and sent a servant to fetch the apothecary. Jane brought Lydia tea and they waited in suspense for Mr. Jones. He finally arrived and examined the now swollen ankle, pronounced it very badly sprained, and told her to stay off it and keep it elevated for several days.

"Several days! But the ball is tonight! Surely there is something that can be done!" Mrs. Bennet cried.

Lydia began to wail again and Mr. Jones sought out Mr. Bennet in his bookroom to inform him of the diagnosis.

The house remained in an uproar for some time until Mrs. Bennet was persuaded to bed by Jane and tended by Hill. Lydia was terribly cross and put out and determined to go to the ball regardless.

"Just think, Lyddie, if you are not there, all the officers will ask after you, and everyone will wonder where you are. If we tell them you are injured, they shall call on you to see if you are better. You will be the topic of everyone's conversation," cajoled Elizabeth.

Lydia looked thoughtful at her sister's suggestion. "There would be a great many callers in a few days," she said slowly.

"Yes, I'm sure they will be very concerned for you," said Elizabeth. It was manipulative and beneath her, but she did not care. If she saw Lydia running through the ball with an officer's saber above her head one more time, she would scream.

"Very well, I shall remain here. But you must tell everyone that it was your fault! I'll not have all the officers thinking I'm clumsy because you run about like a spring colt."

Elizabeth merely smiled and agreed.

Mrs. Bennet stayed in her bed for half an hour until she remembered there was a ball to prepare for; then she dispelled as much energy ordering her daughters and servants about as she had bemoaning her youngest's fate.

Elizabeth had no idea if her fledgling plan would work, but she thought working her way through the wrongs perpetrated those fateful days might yield some positive results. Lydia humiliating their family more times than she could count certainly merited a great wrong in her eyes. She again went to her sister Mary and asked her to play an easier and more cheerful song that evening. It may not bear fruit, but she had made the effort.

She was at a loss on what to do to quiet her mother. Mrs. Bennet was a force to be reckoned with, and once she got an idea in her head, it was impossible to remove it. Elizabeth wondered if it would be better to try to distract others from noticing her instead of trying to curb her mother's behavior. Then, just as she was ready to give up, an idea formed in her mind. It was devious, and foolish, and so very wrong, but as soon as it presented itself, she knew she would pursue it. It was too seductive not to.

After the afternoon meal, Mrs. Bennet said she would rest a quarter hour before dressing for the ball. Elizabeth brought her a cup of tea, and when Hill reported that the mistress was so deeply asleep she could not wake her, Elizabeth looked at her innocently and said to let her mother sleep, for the day had been exciting, and she would surely rouse in time to leave.

She did not.

Mr. Bennet looked in on his wife himself, declared her exhausted and sleeping soundly, and led his daughters to the carriage. Elizabeth couldn't help the tiny smile of triumph that stole onto her face for a moment as they pulled away from Longbourn, sans Lydia and Mrs. Bennet, but any who saw it made no comment, though she noticed her father did look at her with a glint of suspicion in his eye. She smiled sweetly at him and knew his indolent nature would keep him from pursuing it.

Elizabeth enjoyed the ball immensely. She danced with her neighbors and friends, the officers, and both Mr. Darcy and Mr. Bingley. She laughed and smiled so much it bordered on flirtation, but as she did such with men and women alike, no one could claim she meant anything by it and knew it was merely her way.

How wonderful it was to attend a ball without the constant mortification of a vulgar mother and a wild sister! Mary played the song Elizabeth suggested and received sincere applause when she finished. Kitty was significantly more quiet without Lydia to follow, and instead stayed near and imitated the Long girls, whom she had been friends with before Lydia came out and declared them unlikeable, likely for being more elegant than herself, though Lydia never admitted that was the cause.

Relief was Elizabeth's primary emotion when their carriage was not the last one to be called. They stood in the entryway, waiting for the footman to open the door, something like contentment settling about her like a warm blanket. Jane looked tired but happy where she spoke to Mr. Bingley in the corner, Mary had a peaceful expression on her face instead of her habitual frown, and even her father seemed pleased with the evening. Kitty had been invited to tea with the Longs, *alone*, in two days' time, and Elizabeth was hopeful that her family might not be beyond redemption—so long as her mother and Lydia were removed.

"Good night, Miss Elizabeth," said Mr. Darcy, suddenly before her.

"Good night, Mr. Darcy. It has been a pleasant evening. I trust you enjoyed yourself?"

"Yes, it was most pleasant."

"You needn't look so surprised, Mr. Darcy," she teased. He was in great need of teasing—he was entirely too serious.

"I assure you, I am only tired." Before she knew what had happened, he had led her out the newly opened door and to the carriage where he handed her in after Jane, holding her hand a moment longer than necessary. "Goodbye, Miss Elizabeth," he said quietly. It was odd, but there was a note of finality in his voice that would keep her up half the night.

~

Did he know he would leave? Had he known all along? Is that why he had looked at her so consciously? Elizabeth could only conclude that Mr. Darcy may not have planned to leave with Mr. Bingley directly following the ball, but he did plan to leave soon.

She vaguely wondered if that was why he danced with her and spoke so pleasantly to her—he knew he was not coming back and it was his odd way of saying goodbye. She thought on it for a moment, then dismissed it as ridiculous. It was entirely too romantic a notion for Mr. Darcy to entertain, and besides, even if he was the sort of man to wish to carry the memory of a dance with a lady when he knew he was unlikely to see her again, she would never be the lady. He disliked her! He looked at her to find fault! He was constantly arguing with her and insulting her. He ignored her friends and disdained her home. He looked down on her family, though she could admit it was more loyalty than justice that angered her on that front.

Having worked herself up into a good righteous anger, Elizabeth prepared for the ball again. She had stopped her family from humiliating themselves the night before but it hadn't done any good. She had woken up peevish and fitful. She was angry at the world, at

God, at whoever was responsible for placing her in this mess. She was angry at her mother for being loud and embarrassing, at Lydia for being wild and at Kitty for being easily led. She was mad at her father for doing nothing about it, and at herself for being angry over it and caring at all. She was angry at Mr. Darcy more than anyone, for if he knew all along he was going to leave Netherfield and not return, why was she trying to stop them from going? What could she do? If he was determined to leave, Caroline Bingley would follow him, and she was increasingly certain that Mr. Bingley would not be able to stand up to the collective persuasion of his sisters and his imposing friend. He had admitted himself that Mr. Darcy often got the better of him in debates and decisions, and she just knew, deep down somewhere inexplainable, that Darcy would carry the day.

All her efforts were for naught. She was doomed!

It was with these thoughts swirling about her mind that Elizabeth entered the Netherfield Ball that evening. Mr. Darcy asked her for the fourth set as he usually did, and she would have refused him had she not already promised the following dance to Lt. Chamberlain. He smelled vaguely of onions, but he did not deserve to be so unceremoniously left in the lurch.

It was with some pique that she asked him if he believed in premonitions, almost daring him to argue with her.

He was thoughtful for a moment. "Yes, I believe they do exist," he said quietly.

"Do you have personal experience with them?" she asked, being careful to not phrase her words as she had previously in hopes of receiving a different answer.

He looked at her sharply, as if she had just said something outrageous, and replied slowly, "Yes. I have."

The dance separated them then and by the time she had returned to him, so had his usual composure. She looked at him expectantly.

"When my father was training me to manage the estate, we had cause to speak with a brewer who was interested in purchasing grain from Pemberley. He was an affable man, and all our interactions with him had been satisfactory."

Elizabeth danced away and felt her face redden. He was going to tell her that the tradesman was a cheat, and that he, a gentleman, had spotted it. She was on the verge of making a sharp comment when Sir William interrupted them and exclaimed over their dancing and what joy he received from watching them.

"Then we should return to it immediately," Elizabeth interrupted before he could comment on Jane and Bingley. She must remember to position them lower in the dance if she wished to avoid him at future balls. He was one character who never changed even slightly. Not one word was different from the first time she heard them.

Darcy seemed surprised at her remark, but Sir William simply smiled and bustled off, chattering as he went.

"You were saying, Mr. Darcy?" she prompted, more out of a desire to vindicate her assumptions about him than to actually hear his tale.

"Yes, the brewer. Well, as we were approaching the conclusion of our negotiations, my father asked me what I thought of the endeavor. I told him that the brewer was amiable and I knew no wrong of him, but something did not seem quite right. My father encouraged me not to ignore such an instinct and the next day I rode out early to the brewery to see the operation for myself.

"It was several hours away and I arrived midday. I saw some children outside finishing a meagre meal and asked them what they were doing there. They seemed skittish and unwilling to talk, so I dismounted and followed them in."

Elizabeth hated to admit it, but she acutely wanted to know what Mr. Darcy had seen in the brewery. Suddenly, she remembered him saying she was the cleverest woman of his acquaintance. It was a terribly inconvenient time to remember such a nice compliment. It almost made her like him, and it was so difficult to be properly angry with those whom one truly liked.

"Go on," she said encouragingly.

He nodded and continued in a low voice. "The conditions were deplorable. It was dark and filthy, and the workers, down to the last, appeared exhausted and defeated. To my great horror, I saw children, some as young as five, and women who were obviously undernourished. There were things I cannot speak of to a lady, but I will say that there is a mill at Pemberley, and I have visited other such establishments in the past, and nothing prepared me for what I would see that day. The deprivations..." he trailed off and they continued to dance to the lilting music.

Elizabeth was glad it was a slower dance so that she might better hear him. He seemed troubled, so she squeezed his hand when next theirs met. His eyes shot to hers in surprise, and she gave him a small smile of understanding, and hopefully comfort. All her ire had left, so quickly it was as if it had never been, and she was dancing once again with the man who never tread upon her toes or looked down her gown.

"What did you do after your visit?" she asked when his brow had cleared.

"My father sent the magistrate and the more deplorable of his actions were punished by law. Most were not illegal, however, merely cruel. I should have expected no less from a friend of Wickham's."

He said the last so quietly she wasn't sure she heard him correctly. The dance ended and he began to escort her from the floor.

"Forgive me, but I did not hear you properly. You said you should expect no less from whom?"

They were making their way through the crowd toward Elizabeth's mother. She quickly tugged him in another direction, and soon they had gained what little privacy could be had in a ballroom.

He looked at her warily and she looked back, expecting an answer. He seemed reluctant to speak, and he looked away then back at her, and away again.

"Mr. Darcy, did you say this man was a friend of Mr. Wickham's?"

He sighed. "Yes, Miss Bennet, though I probably should not have."

Recklessly, Elizabeth decided she must know all. When would she have another opportunity? And Mr. Darcy would never remember that she had been impertinent and nosy. It was an ideal situation, really.

"What is the nature of your dislike of Mr. Wickham?" she asked boldly.

"It is a private matter, Miss Bennet. I bid you good evening." He bowed stiffly and turned on his heel, leaving the ballroom entirely.

She stood staring after him with a shocked expression on her face. Miss Bingley looked her way and smirked, but Elizabeth ignored her. Mr. Darcy did not return to the ball at all that night, and she knew, with a surety she could not describe, that whatever had happened between Mr. Darcy and Mr. Wickham had been much worse than a disagreement over a living.

Chapter 6

A New Day

As Elizabeth was climbing into the carriage, she thought of something she had yet to try. Every time this happened, she awoke to the following day. Would it be possible to break the mechanism by not going to sleep? She determined to remain awake until the following evening to see what that would accomplish.

Everyone went to bed when they returned to Longbourn, but Elizabeth went to her father's bookroom and selected a book. Then she settled into a chair by the fire and lit a lamp. She read until the sun was bright and went upstairs to prepare for the day. She was dreadfully tired, but she would not give up.

She took her seat in the breakfast parlor and was pleased to notice her family trail in with bleary eyes. Her mother was in no shape to be seen, so she ordered a tray in her room. Lydia and Kitty were discussing the officers they had danced with the night before.

It worked! She did it! It was not Tuesday, but Wednesday. Blessed, wonderful day!

She had a moment of disquiet when she thought of her conversation with Mr. Darcy last night and wondered briefly what he thought of her in the wake of her boldness, but she was too relieved with her success to bother worrying about that. She was walking in the gardens, basking in the joy that was Wednesday, when she realized she still had a problem. The Netherfield party would leave the next day. Jane would be heartbroken.

Perhaps Mr. Bingley would return? She had truly believed he would when she first saw Caroline's letter and heard Jane's excuses for her. But now, after having attended numerous balls where she observed the behavior of the Bingley family and their friend, she could not say that she believed Mr. Bingley would return. In fact, she would be very surprised if he did. Mrs. Hurst and Miss Bingley had made their disdain abundantly clear. Mr. Hurst was a fashionable man and lazy besides. He would not want anyone unfashionable in the family, or anything that would require effort from him, like standing up to those who would decry Bingley's choice.

Charles Bingley had no allies, and Elizabeth was not certain that his character was strong enough to stand alone. His closest friend also appeared against the match, though Mr. Darcy had been surprisingly kind to herself lately. She never ceased to be surprised by him, though she had attended the same ball more than a dozen times now.

She realized with a start that she didn't know how long it had been since this all began. She wondered idly if she would age with all this repetition of time while the people around her remained static, or if she would be twenty forever. There were worse ages to be stuck at, she thought wryly. She had looked particularly gangly at fifteen, and even Jane had been awkward when her height matured before the rest of her. Elizabeth didn't think it was too vain to believe herself to be in very good looks at the moment. Her figure was formed but still firm, her hair was full and soft, and her skin was brilliant and clear. She would always be outshone by Jane, as nearly everyone was, but she knew she was pretty in her own way and thought there were worse things than being perpetually twenty years of age.

But alas, she was no longer stuck, as her plan seemed to have worked. She made her way into the house and was caught by her mother in the entryway.

"Lizzy, Mr. Collins would like to speak with you." She shoved Elizabeth into the drawing room and closed the door quickly behind her.

Elizabeth looked around the empty room and flinched when she saw her cousin standing by the fireplace. She had forgotten this happened the day after the ball. Oh, well. She would just have to suffer through his insulting proposal and refuse him once again. Then she would think of something to prevent the Netherfield party from leaving the following day.

Mr. Collins began speaking, she knew not what of but it was clearly not a proposal yet. She caught the name of his noble patroness in his rambling speech and decided she would try her newfound talent for changing the course of events on her cousin.

"Mr. Collins," she interrupted.

He stuttered to a halt and looked at her in surprise, as if he had forgotten she was there.

"Yes, Cousin?"

"It is impressive that you know just how to behave with Lady Catherine. I'm sure I would not know how to speak to such an exalted person."

"Oh, her nobility will inspire the utmost decorum, I am certain, my dear," he said condescendingly.

She snorted loudly as she had heard Lydia do. It hurt her nose a bit, but the look on Mr. Collins face was well worth it. "La! What a good joke!" Why had she not thought of imitating Lydia sooner? It was sure to repel any man even mildly respectable. "I'm certain she would find me impertinent and headstrong. You know my mother is always complaining about me." She rolled her eyes and flopped into a chair, slumping against the seat and stretching her legs in front of her.

Mr. Collins looked appalled. "Cousin Elizabeth! What are you, I, you," he spluttered and she laughed again.

"Thankfully I shall never meet the grand lady and we shall all be spared the mortification," she said, in something of her usual tone.

He continued to look at her in shock, as if she were a barn cat who had suddenly begun speaking to him.

"She is much too grand for the likes of me, I am sure," she said, in case he was too thick-headed to understand her point. "I wonder if she will get along with your wife, whomever she turns out to be. I could never be a vicar's wife. I would be absolutely horrid at it!" She laughed gaily. "What a joke! Married to a vicar!"

Mr. Collins turned a deep shade of red and she worried for his health for a moment, but then she remembered that he was a young man, and an insulting one besides, and she continued on her chosen path.

Elizabeth rose from the chair and bounded toward the door. "I should like to walk to Meryton and see if there are any officers about. I wouldn't want them to forget me after last night." She smiled mischievously and skipped out the door, leaving an open-mouthed Mr. Collins behind her.

Her mother appeared after she had put on her cloak but before she could make it out the front door.

"Well, what did he say?" asked Mrs. Bennet impatiently.

"He only told me about Lady Catherine, Mama. I cannot imagine why you thought he should have anything else to say."

Her mother gaped at her for a moment and Elizabeth took the opportunity to rush out the door. She walked in the direction of Netherfield, wondering what she could do to make the party remain, at least until Mr. Bingley returned and offered for Jane. Then they could go wherever they liked.

She stopped walking and stared blankly ahead. She was an idiot! Why had she not thought of it before! If Mr. Bingley proposed to Jane at the ball, he could ask Mr. Bennet for his consent and they could announce it that very night. Even if he didn't speak to Mr. Bennet that night, he would surely return to his betrothed! Why had she not tried to get Mr. Bingley to propose before?

She continued walking and wondered how one went about inspiring a man to propose. She knew a lady was supposed to encourage a man she wished for, and discourage those she was uninterested in, but how was that accomplished by someone outside the couple? Could she convince Mr. Bingley to propose? For that matter, why hadn't he already? He had been showing Jane an inordinate amount of attention for two months. Surely he realized he had raised her hopes and the expectations of the neighborhood.

She stopped again. Was that why the entire party followed him to London? They knew he was about to propose and wanted to stop him? Or did Mr. Bingley himself realize he had raised expectations he had no intention of fulfilling and wanted to escape an awkward situation? No, she couldn't believe it of him. Mr. Bingley loved Jane, she knew he did. He simply must!

She shook her head. It didn't matter what she believed. Mr. Bingley had already departed for Town, the spell was broken, and tomorrow would be Thursday and the Netherfield party would depart. She briefly considered sabotaging their carriage again, but besides not thinking it would work for more than a few days, she had barely survived the last effort. She had no desire to relive an experience that brought her so close to having an apoplexy.

Elizabeth wandered towards Netherfield's borders but saw no one about. She wondered what she had been expecting. Did she think Miss Bingley would be walking in the woods and she would beg her not to go because Jane was desperately in love with her brother? She couldn't imagine a scene less likely.

She returned to Longbourn and prepared for dinner, where she sat as far away from Mr. Collins as possible. That man stole wary glances at her the entire evening that she steadfastly ignored. Mary watched Mr. Collins watching Elizabeth with a puzzled expression on her face, and Mrs. Bennet looked between her second eldest and their guest in confusion, wondering what she could do to bring about a proposal if he didn't take the chances she gave him.

Elizabeth was exhausted after having remained awake all night and excused herself shortly after dinner. She put on a soft nightgown and climbed into bed and was asleep in minutes.

She woke early the next morning and decided she would pay a morning call at Netherfield. With Jane. What she would actually do is walk perilously close to the estate and use some excuse to go into the house before the acceptable time to call. She could say she just realized she had left something there when she tended Jane and wanted to get it before they left. Once she was there, she would think of something. Maybe she would secure an invitation for Jane in Town or make plans for them during the festive season. Something, anything!

Once her hair was neatly pinned up, she tiptoed to Jane's room and woke her sister.

"Jane, wake up, dearest. Come for a walk with me."

"Lizzy?" Jane said groggily. "What time is it?"

"It is early, but the day is bright. Let's walk toward Oakham Mount."

"Oh, Lizzy, not today! I am sleepy. And I don't want to tire myself before the ball."

Elizabeth went cold. "What did you say?"

"I said I want to go back to sleep. And we will be up late dancing; we shouldn't tire ourselves out before we even get to the ball."

"Jane," Elizabeth spoke in a thin voice, "what day is it?"

"It is Tuesday, of course." She sat up and looked at her sister. "Are you ill, Lizzy?"

"I feel suddenly unwell." She sank heavily onto her sister's bed.

Jane slid over and opened the blanket to her sister. Elizabeth kicked off her shoes and lay down, her face pale and her eyes blinking frantically.

"Is there anything I can do?" Jane asked, feeling her sister's forehead for a fever.

"No, nothing. I just need a moment. I shall be well soon enough," she said. She stared at the ceiling for several minutes, too shocked to think or plan or speak.

"Sleep will set you to rights," Jane said soothingly. She stroked Elizabeth's hair and hummed softly in an effort to comfort her sister.

There was no comfort to be had, but sleep welcomed Elizabeth into sweet oblivion.

Chapter 7

A Despondent Heart

Elizabeth awoke with a sore heart and a muddled mind. It had not worked. It was once again Tuesday. Wretched, wretched day! She pulled the pillow over her head and decided she would stay as she was for just a little while longer, and feel terribly sorry for herself, then she would get up and do what needed doing.

By the time she dragged herself to the breakfast table, her family had already eaten. She vaguely thought about forming a new plan to break the spell, but she had neither the heart nor the energy for it. She entered the ball that evening looking perfectly dressed and pinned and coifed, but her eyes were dull, and she could find no joy in repeating the same event for the eighteenth time—she had counted the days as she lay in Jane's bed. It was an awful number—eighteen. Had she truly thought just the other day that there were worse days to be trapped in? Or worse ages?

Tosh! At twenty, she had no legal power, and was under the management of her father. And a country ball! At least it was not a public assembly, that was a small mercy, but to spend every evening for the rest of her life dancing with Mr. Collins! Watching her mother brag about her eldest daughter's impending marriage! It was not to be borne!

The music began and she danced the first with Mr. Collins, ignoring everything he said and merely moving away from him when he turned the wrong direction. She considered walking away from him entirely, but she didn't want to deal with her mother's histrionics if she attempted it. Captain Carter, her usual partner for the second set, had yet to ask her, and she took the opportunity to escape. She looked at no one, said nothing, and slipped out a side door. She was familiar enough with the house to find her way to Mr. Bingley's library. It was on the opposite side of the house from the ballroom and card rooms, and she slipped into the dark room silently, grateful for the lack of light and the solitude. She sat gingerly on the sofa near the window and leaned back to look at the night sky through the glass.

Finally, she heard voices in the hall moving toward the dining room at the center of the house. She rose from her comfortable seat and reluctantly left her sanctuary behind. She was coming to the end of the short corridor when she nearly ran into Mr. Darcy.

"Miss Elizabeth!"

"Mr. Darcy." She dipped into a brief curtsey and moved to walk past him.

"May I escort you?" He turned to stand beside her and offered his arm.

She stared at his arm blankly for a moment, then mechanically threaded her own through his crooked elbow.

"Are you well, Miss Elizabeth?" he asked quietly as they approached the dining room. The hall was filling with people and he leaned down to speak in her ear.

To her great mortification, her eyes filled with tears and her throat tightened. He deftly steered them into a side corridor and around a corner, and suddenly they were back near the library again, its door open in front of her.

"Come," he said. He led her into the library and delicately assisted her onto the sofa. "I shall return in a moment."

Before she could respond, he had left the room. She looked about for something to dry her eyes and saw Mr. Darcy's handkerchief on the seat beside her. She wiped her eyes and nose and refolded the fine cloth so the embroidered 'D' was visible. It was nice handiwork. She idly wondered if his sister had stitched it for him, or perhaps an aunt or a cousin. She couldn't imagine Mr. Darcy having a paramour, but she admitted it was a possibility.

She looked up to see Mr. Darcy coming through the door, his features stern. He carried a glass of wine and a plate of food.

"Drink this," he said and handed her the glass and set the plate before her. "You may not feel like eating, but it could help."

"I thank you," she said in a small voice.

He lowered himself slowly into the chair across from her. "Miss Elizabeth, is there anything I might do for you?" he asked softly.

Surprised by his tone, she looked up and answered, "There is nothing anyone can do, I believe. But I thank you for the offer."

He nodded and continued to watch her, and she was struck by how different he looked in the moonlight with his face wreathed in concern. She paused. He was concerned, wasn't he? She chided herself. Of course, he was. He found her, offered his arm, asked after her wellbeing, and led her to privacy when she was in danger of losing her composure. Though she rather enjoyed disliking him, she must admit that he was being very kind to her at the moment.

She was too tired and heartsick to give anything much thought, but as she nibbled on a biscuit from the plate he had brought, she let her mind sort through the many feelings she had towards Mr. Darcy. It had been one thing to dislike him when she only saw him every few days, but it was quite another to maintain such ire on a daily basis. It was exhausting her, that much she could admit.

"You are being very kind to me," she said, unable to keep the surprise out of her voice.

He furrowed his brow for a moment. "Does that surprise you?"

"Yes."

Now he looked shocked. "Why?"

"You don't like me," she said simply. She turned her eyes to her plate and selected a bite of cheese and washed it down with wine.

She finally looked at Mr. Darcy, who was staring at her in what was clearly shock and no little consternation.

"Miss Bennet, I must ask that you tell me where you ever got such a notion."

She shrugged her shoulders, feeling much better for the food and wine. "You were right, the food is helping." She took another bite of cheese and he looked at her incredulously.

"Miss Bennet!"

She returned her attention to him and saw a wildness in his eyes she had not seen there before. She felt odd, as if she were watching herself have this conversation from the other side of the window. She was aware of everything that was happening, but she couldn't bring herself to care overmuch about the outcome of this strange meeting. It would be forgot tomorrow, after all.

"Very well, Mr. Darcy. I have long known you disliked me, from the first moment of our acquaintance at the Meryton Assembly and it was confirmed in subsequent meetings. But I should not speak of such. You have been very kind to me this evening and I thank you."

He looked at her in utter confusion, and she wondered if he needed the wine more than she did. She pushed the glass and plate of food towards him.

"Eat something. It helps." She smiled and he mechanically reached for her glass and sipped out of it, then returned it to the table. She nudged the plate further in his direction and he took some cheese, and then a biscuit.

"Miss Bennet, I like you a very great deal. It astonishes me that you have no notion of it." He spoke calmly but his eyes were bright in the moonlight.

"Forgive me, Mr. Darcy. I must have taken your refusal to dance with me and your disdain of the general neighborhood as marks against me. My mistake," she said lightly and sought out another biscuit.

Darcy bristled. "Miss Bennet, it is you who has refused to dance with me, on two occasions, and I had planned to ask you to dance tonight but you were nowhere to be found."

She was struck silent by the edge in his voice and took a moment to study him. His posture was stiff, and his jaw flexed tightly behind his pursed lips. He was breathing so harshly she could see his nostrils flaring and relaxing in time.

"You are correct, Mr. Darcy, I did refuse you. I believed you to have asked me at Lucas Lodge because Sir William forced the issue, and I assumed you did not truly mean it when you spoke of dancing reels at Netherfield. I apologize for offending you." She spoke dispassionately, in stark contrast to his barely contained emotion. She spared a moment to think on the oddity of the situation, but she truly could care about very little tonight. Her life stretched before her in long, monotonous days and she could not be bothered by something as trivial as Mr. Darcy's feelings about prior dance requests.

"Why would I ask you if I did not mean it?"

"Did you truly ask me? Or did you suggest dancing a reel would be enjoyable, then wait for me to agree with you?"

He replayed the conversation in his mind and finally said, "While I must give credence to your retelling of events, I believe the invitation was clear."

"Was it? I assumed you had meant only to mock me."

"Why would I wish to do that, Miss Bennet?"

"Why indeed, Mr. Darcy?"

He looked at her quizzically and she leaned back on the sofa to look out the window again. "It is a remarkably clear night. We usually see much rain this time of year."

"You truly believe I dislike you, don't you? That is the only reason you could think I would suggest a dance with the intention of mocking you," he stated heatedly. He was clearly unwilling to let the topic lie.

She sighed. "Mr. Darcy, I apologize, truly. If you say you like me well enough, very well, I shall believe you. Does that ease your mind?"

He sat up indignantly and nearly spluttered. "Ease my mind! Miss Bennet," he huffed and ran his hand through his hair.

She felt mildly amused that she had managed to ruffle the unflappable Mr. Darcy, but her amusement was short lived.

"Forgive me, Mr. Darcy. I am in a queer mood tonight. Please, forget I said anything at all."

He looked at her, features set in stone and eyes dark and alive with some great feeling, though she could not say what it was. Finally, she broke the silence. Why not? It was not as if he would remember the conversation later. What could the proprieties matter in a case such as hers?

"I truly am sorry for upsetting you. But you have not behaved as a person who likes me. You stare at me, ignore me, and argue with me every time I see you. What did you suppose I would think?"

"How could I stare at you and ignore you at the same time?"

She huffed. "Before I left Netherfield, we sat in this very library for a half hour together, and you said not a word to me."

"You said nothing to me, either."

"And you argued with me every time I saw you while I was in residence."

"I thought our conversations to be stimulating debates. My apologies if I distressed you."

"You did not distress me!" she cried, finally roused from her ennui. "You only confirmed my previous opinion of you!"

"And what opinion is that, Miss Bennet?"

"That you are prideful and above your company."

He laughed derisively. "And these faults are great indeed! Forgive me if I have not wished to ingratiate myself with every member of the four and twenty families in the neighborhood. I had not thought a person's garrulousness a good indicator of his pride, but perhaps I have been mistaken." He spoke with evident sarcasm and she was indignant at his cavalier response.

"Pride it may not indicate but disdain it certainly does!" He turned his head away, unable to truly deny her accusation and she lifted her chin triumphantly. "You cannot deny it, I see."

He whipped his head towards her and she leaned back from the force of his glare.

"What do you wish from me, Miss Bennet? Do you want me to say I am above the gentlemen farmers and elevated shopkeepers of Meryton? That I could buy and sell this entire town in an instant? That I am the grandson and nephew of an earl, the great-grandson of a marquess, and the son of the largest landholder in Derbyshire? Is that what you wish? For me to give you more ammunition to hurl at me? More pride to accuse me of? I may not be as affable as Bingley, or as friendly with all manner of people as you seem to be, but I am an honest man, and a fair master, and I do not neglect my familial duties as so many others seem to do." He looked at her pointedly and she understood he referenced her father in his final statement.

She flushed in anger and humiliation.

"You may be fair and honest, Mr. Darcy, and perhaps a great many other laudable qualities, but before today, I never saw kindness in you. And that is a very great failing indeed." She stood and moved towards the door. "Please excuse me," she called over her shoulder as she marched through the door.

And she was gone.

Darcy stared after her with his mouth agape and his mind reeling.

Chapter 8

In Which Elizabeth Has a Crisis of Conscience

Elizabeth arose the next morning with a headache and a knot in her stomach. She was first and foremost a lady, a gentleman's daughter, and she had not been brought up to be deliberately rude. She disliked quarreling, a fact many would be surprised to hear of her. She enjoyed a good debate, that was true, but a debate was a discussion of ideas. It sometimes became heated and occasionally evolved into an argument, but it was an argument over an *idea*, a *theory*, a hypothetical situation. It was not about her personally, nor about her opponent.

Her quarrel with Mr. Darcy had been as personal as it was possible to be. She had insulted him and been insulted in turn. She was ashamed of her behavior—it was unladylike and beneath her and she had no excuse but that she was so very tired—of the day, the ball, the endless mundanity of it all. But she should not have said what she did, especially when he had been so kind to her.

What a queer creature she was! She argued with and insulted a man who went out of his way to achieve her comfort and was perfectly polite to men who did nothing for her but offer a dance. She may not like Mr. Darcy very much, but he did not deserve such vitriol from her.

She replayed their argument in her mind and was struck anew by Mr. Darcy's astonishment when she told him she knew he did not like her. He had truly been shocked and denied it vehemently. Could it be? Did he truly like her?

Elizabeth had been forced to reexamine her opinion of many people of late. Her father's indolence had never been as irksome to her as it was now that she had daily reminders in the form of her sisters' wild behavior. Her mother's comportment had always been humiliating, but now it seemed to have a new ability to destroy. She had thought Mr. Bingley all affability and good cheer, but she was beginning to find his lack of conviction to be something of a serious character flaw. Mr. Wickham, once so charming, appeared more cowardly each time she entered Netherfield and he was not within. Perversely, she viewed his lack of attendance as a form of abandonment of herself. He had made himself a friend, charmed his way into her good graces, and colored her picture of Mr. Darcy's character, only to leave her to face that disagreeable man on her own.

Her mind turned again to Mr. Darcy and his odd behavior of late. Since this whole debacle began, she had alternately manipulated him, enjoyed his company, and been angered by him. She hardly knew what to think now. She recalled what an agreeable dance partner he was, and how he could tell a story in a surprisingly engrossing manner. Then she remembered how he had looked down his nose at everyone in the county and not danced with anyone but Bingley's sisters and herself. This memory was followed by his solicitousness towards her last night and his genuine concern for her wellbeing. She could not make him out. It was most vexing!

And of course, she could not forget her own terrible behavior. She was truly ashamed, and though she knew Mr. Darcy would not recall it and that alone rendered an apology unnecessary and likely very strange to the gentleman, she felt she had to make it up to him somehow, for her own conscience if nothing else.

That evening, Elizabeth entered Netherfield with a plan unlike any she had had before. Her goal this night was not to end her relentless repetition of Tuesdays, but to ease her conscience.

She looked for Mr. Darcy when she entered, but he was not in the entryway nor in the ballroom itself. She spoke to Charlotte, then suffered through her dance with Mr. Collins. As he had done every ball to date, Mr. Darcy watched from the side with an expression she had once thought was disdain and dark amusement at her predicament, but now that she was coming to know him better, she wondered at it. If she were to do him the honor of believing he knew his own mind, she must believe that he did in fact like her. She could not fathom why he would—she had done nothing to please him and everything to vex him the entirety of their acquaintance, but perhaps that was the draw. Constant fawning would wear on any sensible person. Or mayhap he was simply too conceited to realize she disliked him. Regardless of his reason for watching her, watch her he did. And for the first time, she decided to use it to her advantage.

At the next turn, when she faced a wall containing no one but gossiping matrons in chairs and Mr. Darcy, she looked him directly in the eye and made a face of great forbearance, then rolled her eyes in the direction of Mr. Collins. She was pleased to see Mr. Darcy start at her silent communication, and as he stalked about the periphery of the room in accordance with her movement down the dance, she continued her little show of faces and expressions and the occasionally mouthed word. She was pleased to see Mr. Darcy fight a smile more than once, and he even enacted a little brow play of his own.

She was asked for the next by Captain Carter. Elizabeth looked down the line and noticed Darcy standing up with Miss Bingley. That lady looked duly impressed with herself and her partner. Elizabeth couldn't help the knowing smirk she sent his way when she tripped past him. She was shocked into missing a step when he gave her a look that could only be described as longsuffering. Her mouth opened wide and her brows rose, and Mr. Darcy grinned at her, for a quick moment only, and it was gone by the time he turned back to face his partner. A tiny laugh escaped her on a rush of air and she clasped hands with Captain Carter in jovial spirits.

So Mr. Darcy wanted to play. Very well. She would play.

Their little game continued through the third set. She danced with Mr. Goulding and he with Mrs. Hurst. At one point, he blew across the feathers adorning Mrs. Hurst's head until they danced and quivered to the music. Elizabeth could not restrain her laugh and her partner smiled proudly, thinking himself the cause of her good cheer. Mr. Darcy looked inordinately pleased with himself by the end of the dance and made his way toward Elizabeth with an expression that could almost be called a smile.

"Miss Bennet, would you do me the honor of dancing the next?"

"Yes, thank you, Mr. Darcy."

He bowed very correctly and left her to await the beginning of the dance.

"Eliza, if I didn't know better, I would say you want to dance with Mr. Darcy," said Charlotte.

"I do. He is a good dancer and a tolerable conversationalist. There are worse partners." She couldn't help sneaking a look at Mr. Collins, which Charlotte ignored.

"I am all astonishment! I thought you quite disliked him," replied her friend.

Elizabeth looked thoughtful for a moment. "I have come to reconsider a great many things of late," she said.

"Well I am glad to hear it. It would not do to slight Mr. Darcy for a man a tenth of his consequence." Elizabeth looked at her in confusion and Charlotte clarified, "I speak of Mr. Wickham, of course. You must have reconsidered indeed if you need such a reminder."

Elizabeth gave her an eloquent look and Charlotte smiled in the superior way she had been doing since they were children.

"You know I did not believe Mr. Wickham's story from the first," Charlotte said matter-of-factly. "Such a thing would be very hard to accomplish, and what would be Mr. Darcy's motive for denying his father's wishes? If the living was mentioned in the will, Mr. Wickham would have had legal recourse. If it was only conditional, I daresay he did not meet the conditions. He has not taken orders, has he? Is he a curate? No! Of course, no rational man would give him a living! Besides," she added with a glint in her eye, "he is entirely too charming to be a vicar."

Elizabeth thought over her friend's statement for a moment. She had great respect for Charlotte's mind and good sense, and now that she no longer viewed Mr. Wickham as a paragon of masculine virtue, she could see the logic in her friend's statements.

"He did share his history with me on very short acquaintance," said Elizabeth thoughtfully.

"Is that not proof in itself that something is amiss? Can you imagine anyone else you know sharing such personal details of themselves in such a way?" chided Charlotte.

Elizabeth ignored the urge to defend Mr. Wickham, which must be said was significantly less powerful than it had been only a few days ago, and thought about what her friend had said. It had been odd of Wickham to do such a thing, and he had said he could do nothing to harm the son for love of the father. But he had harmed Mr. Darcy in her eyes if in no other way. Harmed him quite thoroughly.

She was a little taken aback at her own conclusions and decided to stop thinking of it altogether for the moment. Mr. Darcy came to claim her hand, Charlotte winked at her in what was a disturbingly accurate imitation of Mrs. Bennet, and Elizabeth threw herself into the dance.

"Are you enjoying the ball, Mr. Darcy?"

"Yes, much more than I expected I would," he replied.

She smiled and turned about with the man next to Mr. Darcy, then waited as he did the same with the lady next to her.

"So is it true that you detest balls?"

"Detest is a strong word." She smiled at his response and circled behind him. He watched her path over his shoulder and around to the other side. "Let us say I prefer other forms of entertainment."

"You seemed to be enjoying yourself quite well before our dance." She gave him an impish smile and they joined hands as they sashayed down the line.

"If you truly wish to know something I detest, I will tell you."

She looked at him expectantly. "Go on. I am all agog to hear your answer."

He gave her a small smile and said, "Feathers."

Elizabeth couldn't stop the bark of laughter that leapt out of her mouth, and more than one fellow dancer thought it odd that Mr. Darcy should have made her laugh.

"Will you tell me why you detest such innocuous adornments as feathers?" she asked.

"I'm sure you have noticed I am not a short man," he said seriously.

"I had noticed," she replied, equally serious.

"When worn by a woman shorter than myself—"

"Which is every woman," she interrupted.

"Very nearly. When said woman stands near me, as in a dance, the feathers tickle my face. I dislike it."

He said the last so solemnly, with such a look upon his face that it was all she could do not to burst into laughter in the middle of the ballroom.

"Very well, Mr. Darcy, you win. I cannot argue with your reasoning."

He rewarded her with another of his almost smiles and she returned it brightly. When the dance was through, he led her near the punch table and brought her a drink.

"Mr. Darcy, there is something I would like to discuss with you, of a private nature," Elizabeth said so quietly he had to lean down to hear her. "I know it is untoward, but could you meet me in the library in ten minutes? I mean you no harm," she added with a smile.

He looked at her in surprise, then nodded slowly.

She thanked him for the dance and the refreshment and sauntered off, stopping to speak to an acquaintance before making her way to the library. When she finally entered the room, Mr. Darcy was already standing beside the fireplace, idly poking at the newly lit logs.

She closed the door softly behind her and stepped into the center of the room, still several steps away from him. "Thank you for coming, Mr. Darcy. I know this must seem rather strange to you."

"You certainly have my attention, Miss Bennet," he replied.

She watched him carefully, thinking his posture looked slightly rigid, and his expression was curious, but she could not say whether or not he was suspicious of her motives.

"I wanted to inform you of a rumor that is being spread about you."

His brows rose instantly. Clearly, whatever he had expected her to say, that had not been it. "May I ask the source of this rumor?"

"Mr. George Wickham, though I believe you suspected that."

He nodded slowly. "Yes, it is not the first time he has slandered me."

"Is there any truth to it?" she asked.

"That depends on what he told you. I find that the most convincing lies are those planted with a seed of truth."

"He told me he was promised a living in your father's will but you denied it to him out of jealousy and got away with it due to a technicality with the wording."

"Very succinctly put, Miss Bennet."

She nodded her thanks.

"Do you imagine me the type of man who would deny his own father's will? For that matter, is it likely that I was the only man executing the will? There were others involved; I could not have cheated had I wanted to."

"So there is no truth to it?" she asked keenly.

"Please sit down, Miss Bennet. I shall tell you the truth."

She sat on the sofa near the fireplace and he remained standing, the poker still in his hand, occasionally jabbing at the fire.

"I shall try to be as brief as possible. George Wickham is the son of Pemberley's former steward, a man well respected by myself and my excellent father. When Mr. Wickham Sr. died, my father took on the care of young Wickham. He clothed him, educated him, gave him every advantage. My father was very fond of George. He was a beguiling child and our fathers were trusted friends."

Elizabeth relaxed into the cushions, enjoying the restful atmosphere of the library and the sonorous voice of Mr. Darcy as he told her his history. She could not pinpoint what exactly struck her as different from Mr. Wickham's recitation, but she felt no response was required of her in Mr. Darcy's telling, other than a confirmation of having heard him. Mr. Wickham had wanted constant assurances from his listener—his was a decidedly less relaxing form of discourse.

"George and I were childhood playmates; my father sent him to school with me and we remained friends of a sort for many years. As time went on, it became clear to me that George was not taking his studies seriously. My father had hoped he would go into the church and take on one of the livings in his gift. He intended for George to have a steady income and a home nearby. Being of an age with George, I knew he ought not to be a clergyman, but I did not tell my father of his dissipation. Would to god that I had." He turned away and stabbed at the fire vigorously.

"My father died just after I finished at Cambridge. George had stopped attending after he realized the Darcy name would not buy him good marks in classes he rarely attended. My father's will expressed a wish that George take orders if he desired, and when he was ready and a living came available, George would have it. My father's actual wording stated that he wished me to consider George for a living."

"That is ambiguous indeed," Elizabeth said, one brow raised.

"Indeed. The living at Kympton, the one my father had hoped George would take on, was not available, but we suspected it would fall open in a few years. Whether from a desire not to wait or for some other reason, George declared he did not wish to be a clergyman, and that he would much rather study the law. I was relieved, I admit. He requested money in lieu of the living, and I gave him three-thousand pounds in exchange for him relinquishing all claim to it in the future."

"Three thousand pounds!"

"Yes, and he was given another thousand as a legacy from my father."

"Four thousand pounds!" she squeaked.

"Yes. Quite a sum. A prudent man could have lived several years on such an income. But prudence and George Wickham have never been much acquainted," Darcy said acerbically. "For years I did not see him nor hear of him. I hoped rather than believed he was doing something useful with himself and the money I'd given him. Alas, when the living at Kympton fell open, he heard of it and sent a letter requesting the position. He claimed my father's final wishes and played on our childhood friendship. I refused, of course."

"Naturally!" Elizabeth cried.

Darcy nodded and continued. "He sent me a letter filled with vitriol that does not bear repeating, but I am sure his anger at me was in direct proportion to his distressed circumstances."

"How did he spend so much so quickly? No family, no home to maintain?" she wondered aloud.

"Wickham has never had trouble spending money. It's keeping it that eludes him."

"Was that day in Meryton the first time you saw him since all this happened?"

"No, I'm afraid it wasn't. Last summer, he attempted an elopement with a member of a family well known to me. The girl was but fifteen and persuaded to think herself in love with Wickham, and he with her. His goal, of course, was her dowry of thirty-thousand pounds."

Elizabeth gasped. Fifteen! "How was the plan foiled? Did her family discover it?"

"They did," he said quietly, his arm on the mantle and his back to Elizabeth. "It was discovered just in time. The young lady's spirits have yet to recover. Her confidence has taken a blow. She trusts no one and is terrified of making a mistake."

"So young!" Elizabeth shook her head. "I can't believe it! How can he be so very bad?"

"If you doubt the veracity of my statements, I can send for the paperwork on the will and the living. My cousin is a colonel in the army and was an executor to my father's will and connected to the family of the young girl. He knows all and is an unimpeachable source." He spoke to the floor, his voice low, his body unnervingly still.

"Forgive me, Mr. Darcy. I did not mean to imply that I distrust you. I believe you—utterly and completely. You need not send for anything," she replied, leaning forward. "I was simply expressing my astonishment."

He relaxed slightly and nodded. "Wickham is blessed with happy manners that ensure he makes friends wherever he goes."

"If only he were as good at keeping them," said Elizabeth with heat. "Mr. Darcy, as you began speaking, I pondered on the difference of you telling me your history and Mr. Wickham's recitation. I see now that yours is utterly lacking in manipulation. Wickham watches his target carefully to see what he should say next, where he should press an advantage. He is not informing the listener, but himself. He is gauging their interest and loyalties. It is in every way abhorrent."

"Brava, Miss Bennet," said Mr. Darcy with a look of pride. "I believe you are the first lady of my acquaintance to understand that about Wickham. And so soon after being introduced—you should be impressed."

"I would be more impressed if I had not been taken in in the first place, but I thank you for the compliment, Mr. Darcy."

He nodded again, a small smile gracing his handsome features.

"Now, let us get back to the dance before we are missed," she said, rising from the sofa. "Will you follow in a few minutes?"

"Yes, I shall be directly behind you," he said.

She nodded and turned to walk out of the room, giving him a reassuring smile just before she slipped through the door. He looked back at her with a look in his eyes she could not place. After many hours of tossing in bed, she would decide it was wistful.

Chapter 9

A Little Encouragement

Elizabeth had much to think on the next morning. She couldn't believe she had been so taken in by Mr. Wickham! At least no lasting harm had been done. The more she thought on it, the more she thought it was ridiculous of her—of anyone—to have believed him on such a short acquaintance. She had known him less than a fortnight! She scolded herself roundly, then resolved to think on it no longer.

It was time to focus on the matter at hand. She still saw keeping Bingley in the neighborhood as the best way of ending this cycle, and the best way of keeping him here meant giving him something to stay for, and then something to return for. Something more official than a lady he showed attention to. Something legally binding.

She must find a way to make Bingley propose to Jane this night.

She began with her sister. She helped Jane in every way she could: with her hair, her dress, her rose water. Jane was resplendent. If she could not inspire a man to propose in such a state, no one could. Throughout the day, Elizabeth said anything she could think of to bolster Jane's confidence.

Perhaps Charlotte was correct and Jane should show her affection more readily. Deciding it couldn't hurt, Elizabeth encouraged her sister to be more open with Mr. Bingley, for he was a modest man, and likely to question himself. Jane should leave him in no doubt of her regard. Jane looked at her sister in some surprise, but then said she would encourage the gentleman as best she could.

Elizabeth knew that meant Jane would listen intently, and blush and look at her feet half the night. She would have to intervene on

Jane's behalf.

To that end, Elizabeth put herself in Mr. Bingley's way to be asked for the second dance.

"Now that you have lived here some time, how do you like Hertfordshire, Mr. Bingley?" she asked.

"I like it very well! It is a delightful county."

"I am glad to hear it. Do you think you will buy an estate in the south, or would you prefer to return to the north? I understand you are from there?"

"Yes, I am from Scarborough. I do like the north, and I enjoy being near the seaside. But the south is also very agreeable, and Hertfordshire is an easy distance to London."

"It is that. I have only been to the seaside in Kent. Is it much different in Yorkshire?"

"Oh, yes! The sea is different at nearly every point, I believe."

"You sound like a sailor. Have you missed your calling, do you think?" she teased.

"I might have been a sailor if I did not become so terribly ill on a ship," he laughed. "The sea at Scarborough is a different color, and the light in the north is not the same as it is here."

"Truly? I should like to see that."

"Mayhap you will," he said with a glance at Jane.

"Mr. Bingley," she said haltingly, "forgive my impertinence, but I hope you will one day be the person to show it to me." She glanced her sister's direction quickly before returning her attention to her partner.

He flushed. "I hope that as well, Miss Elizabeth." He paused. She smiled encouragingly. "Do you believe your hope to be shared?" he asked so quietly she almost couldn't hear the words.

"It is. Quite dearly," she answered.

He smiled joyfully and she couldn't help but join him. "Forgive me for speaking out of turn, but I believe you will make an excellent brother."

He flushed again and they both laughed a little nervously. When the dance ended and he bowed over her hand, she squeezed his fingers. His eyes shot to hers and she whispered, "Fortune favors the brave, Mr. Bingley." She winked and left the dance floor to join Charlotte.

"You look flustered," said her friend. "Dare I ask what has happened?"

"Oh, Charlotte, I may have done something very foolish!" cried Elizabeth.

"What did you do?"

"I encouraged Mr. Bingley to offer for Jane."

"That sounds eminently sensible to me. She should snap him up while she can."

Elizabeth groaned.

"Do not feel bad for encouraging your sister's happiness, Eliza."

"I do not fret over that, I only wish I could have gone about it more elegantly."

Charlotte laughed. "Dear Eliza, we cannot all be grand ladies!"

Elizabeth laughed as well and moved to the side to watch the dancing. Mr. Bingley was dancing with Miss Bingley and Mrs. Hurst stood up with Mr. Darcy.

"He does not seem put out," Elizabeth mused.

"He is probably relieved. It is obvious that he cares a good deal for Jane. But he may not move further without some encouragement."

"I certainly gave him that," murmured Elizabeth.

"And she will be glad for it when she is married and well settled." Elizabeth rolled her eyes and Charlotte gave her a look. "Jane cares for Mr. Bingley, that is clear to us who know her, but does he know it? She is so modest, she must do more to help him on."

Elizabeth wanted to argue the point, but knowing what she did about the Netherfield party's future plans, and what she had just said to Mr. Bingley, she really had no right to say anything.

Mr. Darcy asked her to dance the fourth as was his custom, and she was so caught up in watching Mr. Bingley dance with Jane that she said nothing the first several minutes.

"Does something bother you, Miss Bennet?" asked Mr. Darcy.

"Oh, forgive my inattention. I was only distracted. Are you enjoying the evening, Mr. Darcy?"

"Yes, I am. Are you?"

Before she could answer, Sir William passed through the dance and interrupted them to say how much he enjoyed watching them dance and how well they looked. Then he mentioned seeing them dance on another occasion and alluded to the wedding of Jane and Bingley. Elizabeth happened to be looking at Mr. Darcy when Sir William mentioned Bingley's potential wedding and she couldn't miss the expression of shock and disapproval cross his features. He quickly schooled himself back to his usual mien, but she wondered at what he would do. Finally, Sir William left them and they continued in the dance.

"Do you approve?" she asked quietly.

"I beg your pardon?"

"Of Mr. Bingley and my sister. Do you approve?"

She could see she had shocked him with her question and she waited patiently for an answer.

"Bingley is young; I do not know that he is ready to take such a step."

"Then he should not pay her such attentions if he only means to abandon her." She said it before she could think it through, but she could not regret it.

Darcy was surprised and slightly disapproving. "Bingley has no ill intentions. He is friendly and agreeable, and unfortunately that may lead to false expectations."

"There's a word for men like that," she said with a look.

He stared back at her and she danced around him and patiently waited as he turned about with the lady on her right.

"You think him capricious?" asked Darcy when they came back together.

"Is he not? He has shown Jane an inordinate amount of attention. He has raised her hopes and the expectations of her family and the entire neighborhood. He should not have engaged her heart if his intentions were not honorable."

Darcy looked surprised at this and opened his mouth as if he wanted to say something, but no words came out.

Elizabeth continued. "He may run off to London or Scarborough or elsewhere when he is through here, but this is Jane's home county. If he abandons her, she will be humiliated and pitied by all her neighbors. Everywhere she goes they will whisper about her behind fans and fall quiet when she enters a room. I have seen it happen before. Jane's sweet disposition will be exceedingly distressed by such a situation, and her distress will be amplified by knowing she has lost the only man she ever truly cared for."

Darcy was staring at her silently and she realized she had said much more than she intended to say. "Forgive me, Mr. Darcy. My tongue ran away with me."

"There is nothing to forgive, Miss Bennet. You care for your sister and wish to see her happy. That is commendable."

She nodded and they danced in silence. "I know he could do better," Elizabeth said as they waited at the top of the line. His brows rose to his hairline and she thought this must be her night for shocking poor Mr. Darcy. "In terms of wealth, certainly, and connections. But she is a gentleman's daughter, and Longbourn has been the seat of the Bennets for seven generations."

He nodded in acknowledgement of her statement and she continued in a low voice. "Jane herself is the sweetest, kindest, most amiable woman who ever lived. Any man who secured her heart and hand could never repine. I have seen her in every mood, in every climate and situation, and I have never seen another with such patience, such gentleness in the face of provocation. She will be a very good wife, I have no doubt of it, and an exemplary mother."

Her cheeks were flushed with the defense of her sister, and he could not but look at her admiringly.

"I understand you perfectly, Miss Bennet. Bingley will hear no words of censure from me."

She smiled brilliantly at him and he bowed slightly. The music came to a stop and he led her off the floor, but not before she saw Bingley leading Jane out onto the balcony on the other side of the room. She said a quick prayer that he would propose and joined Charlotte.

"Is it happening?" asked Charlotte, her eyes also on the balcony door Bingley had led Jane through.

"I hope so," replied Elizabeth.

They watched the door nervously, Elizabeth grasping her friend's hand and feeling Charlotte's reassuring squeeze in return.

Finally, ten long minutes later, Jane stepped into the ballroom, flushed and smiling, an equally bright Bingley trailing behind her. Elizabeth caught her sister's eye and Jane made her way to them.

Jane grasped Elizabeth's hands tightly and cried, "Oh, Lizzy, I am the happiest creature in the world!"

"Did Mr. Bingley propose?" asked Charlotte.

"He did!" answered Jane. She took Charlotte's hand in hers and pulled her friend and sister closer. "Oh, if everyone could be so happy!"

"I am happy to see you happy, dearest. Has Mr. Bingley gone to Papa?" asked Elizabeth.

"Yes! He said he couldn't wait another moment. Oh, how shall I bear such joy? If only there was such a man for you, Lizzy, I wouldn't wish for anything else."

"Do not worry for me, Jane. I am content to wait for my own Mr. Bingley."

Soon enough, Mrs. Bennet had heard the news and let out a great shriek that rose above the sounds of the musicians. The entire ballroom was aware of the engagement within minutes, and Mr. Bennet made a formal announcement at the supper that evening.

Elizabeth went to bed peaceful and happy, believing she had finally accomplished what she set out to do.

She awoke the next morning to the shrill sound of her mother screeching, and waited patiently for her door to fly open and her mother to barge in.

"Wake up, Miss Lizzy! It will take Sarah ages to arrange all that hair." Mrs. Bennet bustled out as quickly as she had come in.

Elizabeth groaned and pulled the blankets over her head.

Chapter 10

If You Can't Beat Them, Laugh at Them

If Mr. Bingley proposing to Jane was not the key to this riddle, what was? Elizabeth pondered that question the whole of the day following Bingley's proposal. She had come to no grand conclusions by that evening's ball, and she allowed events to proceed as they usually did with no interference from her. Jane blushed, Mrs. Bennet crowed, Lydia ran wild, and Mr. Bennet ignored them all. Elizabeth watched her family humiliate themselves with a jaundiced eye. She went about her dance with Mr. Collins mechanically, then accepted Captain Carter's request for the second set.

Kitty was dancing further up the line with Mr. Denny. Odd, but for the first time, Elizabeth noticed that her younger sister was not giggling wildly or behaving like a bird someone had inadvertently let inside, flying around madly and running into windows. Kitty blushed and smiled and looked down a great deal, only to peek back up at Mr. Denny, who seemed to be smiling rather broadly at her. *Interesting.* Elizabeth filed this information away for further examination and returned her attention to her partner.

She was speaking to Charlotte for what felt like the hundredth time when Mr. Darcy requested the fourth set. She smiled kindly, accepted, and pointedly ignored Charlotte's barely-veiled comments on Mr. Darcy's attraction to her. He may like her, but *attraction* was another thing altogether.

Elizabeth's mind was so distracted that she barely spoke to her partner. They were more than halfway through the dance when Elizabeth looked up and noticed Mr. Darcy watching her with a frown.

"Are you well, Mr. Darcy?"

"I was going to ask the same of you, Miss Elizabeth."

She looked surprised, then sighed and allowed her shoulders to drop for a moment. "I am tired, that is all. I find myself lacking the patience such an occasion requires."

His mouth lifted slightly on one side. "I often find myself in the same position."

She couldn't help but smile at his confession. He smiled briefly in return and they danced in silence.

When the dance ended, he bowed and said, "I hope my company wasn't too taxing on your forbearance, Miss Elizabeth."

"The company was excellent, I thank you, sir," she said with a curtsey.

He nodded in acknowledgement of the compliment, though she fancied he looked slightly surprised.

Soon enough it was time for dinner and the throng of guests made their way into the hall and on to the dining room. Several guests had consumed too much punch and as a result, the group that wandered into dinner was rather more relaxed than what would usually be seen. Mrs. Bennet may have over-indulged, but her usual conversation was so vulgar and disjointed it was hard to tell. The intensity in volume was the only indicator of her state of inebriation, and Elizabeth sincerely hoped it was the excitement of the event that had her so animated.

In Lydia's case, however, it was embarrassingly clear that her over-loud speech, her incessant giggling, and the fact that she actually ran through the front hall with an officer in hot pursuit was the result of an overconsumption of Bingley's strongly flavored punch. Elizabeth groaned and closed her eyes against the sight. Mr. Chamberlain, the smell of onions wafting behind him, chased her youngest sister through the hall past Elizabeth and a dozen of their closest neighbors where they waited to enter the dining room, Mr. Chamberlain calling out for her to stop and give him back his sword. Lydia laughed madly and ran faster, her dress flying up nearly to her knees.

Filled with a deep desire to stop this madness—and a temporary release of all bonds of decorum and polite behavior—Elizabeth waited for Lydia to approach her, then calmly stepped away from her neighbors, directly into her sister's path. Lydia saw the obstacle in her way and swerved to her right, and Elizabeth just as swiftly stretched out a leg in her sister's direction. Lydia opened her mouth wide in silent surprise (the quietest she had been all evening), and flew into the air, hovering horizontally for a brief moment before landing flat on the ground in a spectacular heap of fine muslin, an abundance of lace, and a (thankfully) dull sword.

Mr. Chamberlain was directly behind her and narrowly avoided tripping over her prone form. He gallantly helped her up, re-sheathed his sword, and inquired if Lydia were well, to which she replied, between hiccups and uncontrollable giggles, that she was jolly well, but did anyone else see her sister Elizabeth? She could have sworn she had seen her just before she fell, but by the time she was on her feet and put to rights, Elizabeth was gone.

He could not answer her, and the neighbors that had witnessed the event chose to ignore her and pretend they hadn't seen anything, except of course to tell everybody else at the ball exactly what had happened—with a few tasteful embellishments.

Elizabeth smiled to herself from her position around the corner. She felt no remorse. Lydia was unharmed, and would be even less harmed tomorrow, but Elizabeth herself felt better. Surely that was worth something. She walked away, ignoring her neighbors' questions and greetings, and made her way to a side terrace. Torches had been lit at intervals along the stone railing and the only other occupants, a couple she didn't recognize, went inside a few minutes after she arrived.

Elizabeth leaned against the stone, looking up at the dark sky. She felt a small measure of harmony at her own tininess in a vast world and felt vaguely comforted by the time she re-entered the house.

Caroline Bingley was in the hall and approached Elizabeth. Likely because she had sensed Elizabeth's hard-won peace of mind and wished to obliterate it.

"Miss Eliza," she slithered closer and Elizabeth couldn't stop the sigh that raised her shoulders and sank them back down again.

"Miss Bingley."

"Your family certainly seems to be enjoying the ball," she said with a wickedly gleeful look on her face.

Mrs. Bennet's voice rose above the noise of the crowd and Elizabeth cringed, as Miss Bingley had intended. Not wanting to speak to her a moment more, Elizabeth looked away, feeling all the rage and humiliation and despair she had felt over the last days running through her body until she was full of it from her toes to the top of her head. A cup of punch was abandoned on a nearby table and Elizabeth stared at it, her eyes fixed on the colorful liquid. Caroline continued to drone on, something about Christmas in Town and spending time with the Darcys, the note of triumph evident in her voice, even if the words were obscured.

Elizabeth could take it no longer. She reached for the glass of punch and held it in front of her, stretched towards Miss Bingley, and tipped it calmly onto the lady's dress. Miss Bingley did not stop talking until she felt the sticky liquid seeping through her bodice and onto her skin, when she finally turned her attention to her companion. Miss Elizabeth bore a serene expression, her eyes fixed steadily on her motions as she drained the glass over Caroline's new silk gown.

Miss Bingley gasped. She squeaked. She huffed and cried, "Why you little!" before stopping herself and storming towards the stairs as quickly as she could while keeping the front of her dress concealed. Elizabeth allowed herself a small smile of satisfaction, then set the glass back on the table and went to find her father. She had had enough of the ball and would call for the carriage to take her home. She was nearly into the dining room when Mr. Darcy stepped out the door and into her way.

"That is one way to silence a loquacious conversation partner."

She looked up at him, startled at his sudden appearance. Was he smirking? His lip was twitching in the corner and if she didn't know better, she would say Mr. Darcy was trying not to laugh.

"Forgive my display, Mr. Darcy. I found I could listen no longer. Excuse me, I must find my father."

"He is just there," replied Mr. Darcy, pointing to a corner of the dining room.

"Thank you. Good evening," said Elizabeth.

"Are you leaving?" he asked.

"Yes, I've had enough merriment for one night."

"May I see you home?"

She looked at him in surprise, and indeed, he seemed surprised to have made the offer.

"Thank you, Mr. Darcy. I shall be well in the carriage on my own." Feeling a burst of mischief, she added, "Though it is a beautiful night. It is a pity I may not walk home."

"Yes, a pity," he said thoughtfully.

He looked at her in such a way that she half thought he would offer to walk her home in the moonlight, but she knew he was too proper to let such a suggestion escape his lips, even if he had been improper enough to think it. Then again…

"It is too bad I have not a proper escort. I could ask Mr. Collins, but that would rather defeat the purpose."

Darcy looked at her in question.

"What is the purpose of a night stroll if not peace and quiet?" she teased.

His eyes flared, thoughts of why one might go on a night-time stroll with a young woman practically dancing across his features, and she realized too late what she had inadvertently referred to. She colored.

"Excuse me." She made her way to her father, whispered in his ear, and was soon back in the hall. "I will call for the carriage. It will return for my family."

She didn't know why she was explaining herself to Mr. Darcy, but he was looking at her in that way he had always done, but more intently somehow, and she found herself nervous under his scowl.

"Allow me."

Before she could answer, he had removed to the entryway to call the carriage. Elizabeth stepped into the dining room again, caught Jane's eye and waved goodnight, then found her cape in the cloakroom. Mr. Darcy was awaiting her just outside the door and took the cape from her hands, draping it around her shoulders with surprising deftness.

"Thank you," she said. He was doing it again. Staring at her so fiercely she thought she had something on her face. "Why do you glare at me if you do not dislike me?" she blurted.

He blinked. Clearly, he had not expected such a question. "I do not glare at you."

"Permit me to know when I am being glared at, Mr. Darcy."

"I may… look intently… sometimes. But I do not glare! Certainly not at you."

"Very well. Then why do you look intently at me?"

He opened his mouth. Then snapped it shut. He repeated this motion twice more before she moved past him into the entryway.

"The carriage should be ready now."

He followed her mutely through the entryway and out the front door. The carriage had just rolled to a stop and a Netherfield footman opened the door. Elizabeth descended the front steps, Darcy just behind her.

She stopped in front of the carriage and turned to face him. He reached for her hand and she placed hers on his delicately and allowed him to help her into the carriage. For a moment, she was on the step, her head slightly higher than Mr. Darcy's.

He still held her hand, and she stared at him, as ferociously as he had ever stared at her. She felt the pressure on her hand increase, and slowly, painstakingly slowly, he raised her hand to his lips. She felt the pressure through her light evening gloves and warmth suffused her, traveling up her hand and through her arm, flushing her cheeks and rising gooseflesh on her skin. Her lips parted in a gasp and he raised his eyes, his head still bent, and smiled. His smile was small, and artless, and nearly boyish, but somehow retained a hint of the intensity of his usual looks.

She met his gaze as he raised his head and she refused to look away or be cowed by him. He seemed to recognize her stubbornness and smiled again, a smile of understanding and amusement, and a little bit of indulgence and something else she couldn't define, though she would later learn its name well enough. She grinned back, and desiring to surprise him, she swiftly leaned forward and planted a kiss on his cheek.

She achieved her object. Mr. Darcy's eyes widened instantly. His cheeks turned a brilliant red visible even in the moonlight. His hand dropped uselessly to his side. She smiled winsomely, called goodnight, and ducked into the carriage. She pulled the door closed behind her and called for the driver to move on before Mr. Darcy remembered to blink.

Chapter 11

A Taste of Freedom

Elizabeth awoke the next morning all aflutter. She had never felt so daring, so free from all restraint. She had met her impulses with action and the effect was liberating. Her mother's shrill cries could not disturb her today—she was too high to be brought down.

She had kissed a man—Mr. Darcy!—in front of Netherfield. She had shocked him, that was clear, and she had no recollection of the footman's position during her reckless actions. He may have been standing only a few feet away, she really couldn't say. Oh, how wild she had been!

And she had poured punch down Miss Bingley's dress! And tripped her own sister in the hall! What if Lydia had landed on the saber and it had cut her? She knew she should be concerned about these things, but she could not truly care. She had never felt so free.

And she had kissed Mr. Darcy!

~

Her ebullient mood was not to last. Kitty and Lydia had started arguing over who owned the pale pink ribbon that happened to match each of their dresses for the ball. Kitty recalled purchasing it herself, and Lydia insisted it suited her coloring better and therefore must belong to her. Taking a deep breath, Elizabeth stepped into the room and tried to solve the quarrel. Seeing it couldn't be done without the magistrate, she took the key from the lock, and without either sister noticing, left the room and closed and locked the door behind her.

She was on the stairs when Lydia began pounding on the door.

Elizabeth paused and yelled back to her that she would unlock the door when they began acting more like proper young ladies and less like feral children. She smiled to herself when the sound of feet stomping and what sounded suspiciously like a growl followed her down the stairs.

Luckily, the breakfast room was far enough away that their cries could not be heard and she ate her meal in peace. When it was just she and Jane at the table, mercifully, she said, "You know, Jane, I really think you ought to be more forthcoming with Mr. Bingley."

Jane looked at her in confusion. "What do you mean?"

"I mean that you are so reserved, a person who does not know you well could mistake your serenity for indifference."

Jane looked worried and perplexed at the notion.

"I do not mean to trouble you, I only wish to encourage you to be more demonstrative with Mr. Bingley." At Jane's look of alarm, she added hastily, "I am not suggesting anything unseemly, of course. Merely that some encouragement might not go amiss."

Jane smiled nervously and nodded, saying that she would try. Elizabeth said that was all that she could ask and left for a long ramble in the garden.

When she returned to the house, she could not hear Lydia screaming and assumed someone had gotten a key from Hill and let them out. Not caring enough to find out, she went to the music room and played her favorite pieces, then found Sarah and had her hair put up in a new style she had considered but had never been brave enough to try for fear it would make her face look too thin. She did not have Jane's full cheeks or Lydia's round face, and it had been commented on enough that she was well aware of it.

Somewhat surprisingly, she was well-pleased with the new style and took herself off to show it to her mother. Mrs. Bennet was happy to see her most troublesome daughter ready for the ball hours in advance and happily drank the tea Elizabeth brought her, requesting her daughter leave her for a nap shortly after. Elizabeth closed the door behind her with a smile and made her way to Mary's room.

She once again entreated her sister to play music more suited to her abilities and went a step further by asking Mary to allow Elizabeth to arrange her hair. Mary protested, but Elizabeth insisted. Once Mary's hair was in order, and very becoming, too, Elizabeth wouldn't rest until her plainest sister was wearing Jane's old ball gown and attaching shoe roses to her dancing slippers. Mary was a little uncomfortable with the change in her appearance, but Elizabeth was so complimentary and persuasive, and Jane was so pleasantly surprised when she saw her younger sister, that Mary decided to allow them to make her over if it brought them such pleasure.

Elizabeth finally peeked into Lydia and Kitty's room, which was still locked. She found the room empty and was unsurprised to find out that after two hours of whining and hoping someone would release them, Lydia had climbed out the window and down the trellis. Her sister was nothing if not determined. *If only she would direct it towards more appropriate pursuits…*

Kitty had followed her younger sister and they had taken themselves directly to their father's bookroom to complain of their ill treatment by Elizabeth. Mr. Bennet laughed heartily and told them that they should have been locked in for squabbling ages ago, and if he had known they were so resourceful, he would have made better use of them before today. Both girls were terrifically put out, especially Lydia who felt herself very ill used, and she wasted no time hunting down Elizabeth and berating her soundly.

Elizabeth listened with one ear as she made her way through the house, Lydia hot on her heels and complaining loudly. When she was on the stairs, a few steps up from the bottom, Elizabeth turned abruptly and gave Lydia a small shove, like they had done when they were children, and said she had heard enough. Lydia lost her balance and stumbled, as Elizabeth had intended.

Her ankle was twisted and she cried out in pain and accusation at her elder sister, yelling loudly that Elizabeth had shoved her completely unprovoked.

"I would never push you down the stairs, Lydia. How could you say such a thing?" defended Elizabeth when Lydia accused her in front of Jane and Kitty.

They helped Lydia to the divan in the drawing room and Jane had the apothecary sent for. Mrs. Bennet was sleeping and couldn't be roused, but Mr. Bennet looked at the ankle perfunctorily and told her to put ice on it and keep it elevated, as Mr. Jones was likely to tell her. Lydia continued to pout and complain of her ill treatment and told anyone who would listen that Elizabeth had tried to murder her.

"You mustn't say such things, Lydia," said Jane reproachfully.

"Really, Lydia. You make it sound as if I tried to break your neck!

If that had been my intention, I would have pushed you from the top." Elizabeth huffed, appearing thoroughly affronted at being so accused, and said, "Why ever would I wish to do such a thing?"

Elizabeth was the picture of innocence and Lydia looked at her warily, then whispered to Kitty that she must not leave her alone with Elizabeth before she was able to run, no matter what.

Elizabeth hid her amusement in the entire affair and finished preparing for the ball. She borrowed her mother's pearl necklace, the one that had belonged to her grandmother, and happily fastened Lydia's shoe roses onto her dancing slippers. Lydia wouldn't have need for them while her leg was propped up in the drawing room. She hummed as she wrapped her cloak about her and stepped into the carriage.

Elizabeth entered the ball determined to do what she wished and nothing else. She began with Mr. Collins. She approached him and boldly stated that she would not dance the first with him, with no explanation, and directed him to her friend Charlotte or her sister Mary, both of whom were free for the first set and found his company manageable. He gaped like a fish and she left him standing alone before he could collect himself enough to reply.

She snuck into the dining room and stole a marzipan flower from a tray, giving the footman who saw her a wink before leaving the room. She walked out to the terrace and nibbled on her treat, watching the stars in the ever-darkening sky, the music from the ballroom a perfect background to her musings.

"Here you are," said a familiar voice.

"Charlotte! You look lovely this evening!"

Charlotte smiled. "Thank you. Is that a new gown? It is very fine," she lightly touched the lace at Elizabeth's sleeve.

"It is, thank you." *How new it can be after wearing it to twenty balls, I know not.*

Elizabeth handed Charlotte a bit of the marzipan she had pilfered from the dining hall. Charlotte took it without asking why she had it in the first place and they spent the first set of the evening on the terrace, looking at the stars, and talking about nothing as close friends are wont to do. Elizabeth sighed happily. This was a much better way to spend the evening than dodging Mr. Collins' plodding feet.

She returned to the ballroom shortly before the first set ended to see Mr. Collins dancing with her sister Mary. Mary actually looked pleased to be dancing with him. Elizabeth didn't know if it was because Mary was happy to be dancing the first set at all, or if she particularly liked dancing with Mr. Collins. Either way, Elizabeth was glad it was someone other than herself having her toes tread on.

She danced with Captain Carter and flirted shamelessly, then repeated the process with another officer directly after him. She was enjoying herself immensely and when Mr. Darcy sought her out for the fourth set, as he always did, she smiled brightly and told him she would be delighted to dance with him. He seemed surprised by her eager agreement but hid it with a correct bow before leaving her to await the set with Charlotte.

"I think he admires you, Eliza," said Charlotte.

"You may be right, though I cannot be sure," replied Elizabeth.

Charlotte was clearly shocked that her young friend would agree so easily. "You are the only woman he has asked to dance outside his party," said Charlotte in support of her assertion.

"That is true," said Elizabeth thoughtfully. "Tell me, Charlotte, you have brothers. How does a woman know a man admires her? Truly admires her," she amended, "and not just to look at while dancing?"

Charlotte was surprised, but living up to her reputation for practicality, she quickly became thoughtful and said, "I do not know from personal experience, but what I have gleaned from observation is that a man who admires a woman is more respectful than one who merely looks upon her for his own pleasure. He would be solicitous of her, and care for her comfort, and treat her with respect."

Elizabeth was quickly turning a bright shade of pink. Mr. Darcy had done all those things for her, at one ball or other. "Would he confide in her, trust her with intimate details of his life?" she asked.

"Yes, I think he would. It seems fitting, don't you think?"

Elizabeth nodded but said no more. Could it be? Did Mr. Darcy admire her? *Truly* admire her? What was she to do with such information? She could hardly act on it.

But she could confirm it.

Mr. Darcy collected her for their dance and she decided she must know the truth. She smiled, she flirted mildly, and when his responses were not quite what she desired, she teased him. She kept this up until she had prompted three of his barely there smiles and congratulated herself for her effort.

"You should smile more often, Mr. Darcy. You are so handsome when you are not glowering, and even more so when you smile."

He flushed at the praise and she would have felt embarrassed at her boldness had she not known it would all be forgot by morning.

"I do not glower, Miss Elizabeth," he replied, but she fancied his heart wasn't in it.

"Do you not? Then please, sir, forgive my misapprehension." She passed very near him in the figure and danced a small circle around him, keeping her eyes on his as he tracked her movements around him, looking over his shoulder to keep her in view. "It must have been my mistake." Her smirking lips and dancing eyes were at odds with her words, and she thought that if he had not been glowering before, he certainly was now.

He said nothing for a few minutes, and she kept her eyes on him, in some fashion or other throughout the next several movements.

"Mr. Darcy, what would you call the expression you are wearing now?" she asked archly.

His lip twitched and he said, "I do not believe I have an expression at the moment, Miss Elizabeth. I believe my features to be neutral."

"Ah, I think I have discovered the point of our disagreement."

He raised his brows.

"What you consider to be a neutral expression, I consider to be glowering." She smiled in satisfaction. "There, that was easily settled."

He stared at her for a moment, then said, "As I have already told you, Miss Elizabeth, I do not glower."

"Of course not, sir. You only look intently," she teased.

His surprise was evident and she tripped away to turn about with the ladies, glad the dance had moved them apart. When she returned to him, he had another curious half-smile on his face and she grinned at him, feeling in charity with his feelings for a change. The dance ended shortly after and she took the opportunity to squeeze his hand when he bowed over hers. He looked at her in question and she gave him what she hoped was a reassuring smile. She was met with a look of pleasure, followed swiftly by what appeared to be alarm.

He left her with her sister and was not seen again for the remainder of the evening.

Chapter 12

In Which There Are Many Quarrels

Elizabeth was decided: Mr. Darcy admired her, at least somewhat. How much he admired her she could not say. What he planned to do about his admiration was even less clear. She had thought her behavior the evening before would encourage him or bring him some relief, but it had seemed to have the opposite effect.

After much thought and analysis, she came to the conclusion that one of two things had happened. One, she had been mistaken and Mr. Darcy did not admire her, and was therefore disturbed by what he perceived to be her unwelcome admiration. She thought this unlikely—after all, Miss Bingley showered him with unwelcome admiration daily and he did not seem to mind it—but she could not dismiss it as a possibility.

The second option was that Mr. Darcy *did* admire her, but he had no intention of acting on his feelings. Thus he would be distressed when the object of his affection appeared to reciprocate his admiration, making the eventual leaving of her all the more difficult. She thought this scenario far more likely given what she knew of his character. Mr. Darcy was a dutiful man and from an illustrious family. He would not marry hastily or unwisely.

She also recalled her thoughts when the ball repetition began: that Mr. Darcy asked her to dance to give himself one last memory of her. She had dismissed it as absurd and too romantic a notion for such a staid gentleman, but after spending numerous evenings in his company, it no longer seemed out of the realm of possibility. She also recalled how he had said goodbye to her as if he thought to never see her again. If he was remaining at Netherfield, why would he behave so? She concluded he intended to leave Hertfordshire soon and not come back, and that it was possible she had more than a little to do with his hasty retreat.

Elizabeth knew she was a vain creature; she was not wholly unaware of her own nature. She could admit to herself that the idea of Mr. Darcy feeling such a strong regard for her that he felt the need to flee the county was a bit extreme—if rather flattering to herself. It was more than a little preposterous. But she could not quiet the whisper in her heart that told her he was leaving because of her.

~

Elizabeth had no more answers by the time they arrived at Netherfield. She felt all the honor of having inspired tender feelings in such a man, but she also felt the insult of him not wishing to act upon them. She understood he was above her in position and fortune, but she was a gentleman's daughter, from a respectable family. She was not a scullery maid! The match would be a trifle unequal and there would be some talk, but it would not be overwhelming if everyone saw how well they got on and the affection between them.

She would have been surprised at her own turn of mind if she had not already grudgingly admitted to herself that she had some manner of tender feelings for Mr. Darcy as well. He had been a comforting friend throughout this trial, and her dance with him was often the best part of this never-ending day. Alas, she knew she was in exceptional circumstances and were it any other day, or days, as it were, she would likely feel differently. She did not take her feelings very seriously. When time returned to its usual customs, so would she.

Her thoughts were interrupted by Lydia's shrieks as she pulled Kitty into the ballroom where she had just spotted Mr. Denny. Elizabeth sighed, wishing she had dosed her sister with laudanum before they came. It was always the same, and yet she never stopped being embarrassed by it. She would have thought she would be immune to her family's behavior by now.

Her mother was loudly exclaiming to Lady Lucas about the ball being in Jane's honor, and Elizabeth lost her patience. She marched up to her mother and said she needed her urgently, then practically dragged her into the ladies' cloak room which was mercifully empty.

"Lizzy, what has come over you? We are missing the ball!"

"Mama, you must curb your tongue."

"What?" Mrs. Bennet cried.

"You are loud and vulgar and speaking of things which should not be said in public. You are embarrassing Jane and me and making uncomfortable everyone of sense who hears you," Elizabeth stated matter-of-factly.

Mrs. Bennet spluttered. "How dare you speak to your mother so! I am perfectly behaved! Who are you to tell me how to conduct myself?"

"I am a gentleman's daughter," said Elizabeth in hard tones.

Mrs. Bennet gaped. Her eyes bulged. Her hands fluttered uselessly.

Elizabeth took mercy on her and gentled her voice, saying, "Mama, I do not wish to injure you, but surely you are well enough acquainted with Jane's disposition to realize that such talk only embarrasses her. If she is blushing for her family all night, how will she spare attention for Mr. Bingley?"

Mrs. Bennet had begun to protest that she was not at all embarrassing when Elizabeth's last statement intruded on her indignation.

"Things are done differently in London, and the Bingleys and their friends are accustomed to more refined and quiet society. You must temper your voice, Mama. And you mustn't brag about things that have not happened. You may offend Mr. Bingley and it could hinder him paying his addresses to Jane."

Mrs. Bennet huffed and rolled her eyes, but she did so want Mr. Bingley for a son-in-law.

"Your impertinence will do you no favors, Miss Lizzy," scolded Mrs. Bennet. She sighed. "Very well. I will modulate my voice. Not because it is correct," she added hurriedly, "but for Jane."

Elizabeth impulsively kissed her mother's cheek. "Thank you, Mama."

They rejoined the others and Elizabeth looked worriedly to where Lydia stood in a circle of red coats, flirting shamelessly and leaning forward to better expose her bosom, framed and displayed in a shockingly low gown. Had it been that low at Longbourn? She looked to her mother, but that good lady had already gone off to speak to Mrs. Goulding without a glance at her youngest child's antics. She knew it was too much to ask for her mother to behave herself *and* control Lydia.

Knowing she had nothing to lose, and possibly much mortification from which to save herself, she approached Lydia and excused them from the soldiers, taking her sister by the arm and leading her to the other side of the house.

"Lizzy, where are we going?" asked Lydia loudly.

Elizabeth only pulled her faster until they reached the library.

"Lydia, I have a favor to ask of you."

Lydia looked at her expectantly.

"I want you to behave perfectly tonight, with the utmost decorum, and not run about wildly, or drink too much punch, or laugh too loudly. And do not flirt with every officer present."

Lydia looked at her with wide eyes, then burst into laughter. "Lord, Lizzy! What a good joke! Why did you really bring me here? Is there some sort of surprise?"

Elizabeth took a deep breath. "Mr. Bingley and his friends are accustomed to a different style of behavior in their circles. Jane cares for Mr. Bingley very much and we don't want to spoil her chances."

"Mr. Bingley is so in love with Jane he wouldn't care if she were the apothecary's daughter," said Lydia flippantly. "Everybody knows that."

Elizabeth gritted her teeth. "Mr. Bingley is not the only one affected by his decision or indeed influencing his choice. Surely you do not think Miss Bingley is as enamored with Jane?"

"I do not think Miss Bingley is enamored of anyone," Lydia looked thoughtful for a moment, "well, perhaps herself."

Elizabeth stifled a laugh.

"But I don't see how my behavior affects Jane's chances. I am only having fun! I am doing nothing wrong," declared Lydia.

"Lydia, you are making a fool of yourself, only you are too young to realize it. The officers spend every second moment looking down your gown, and even if they did harbor tender feelings for you, none of them makes enough money to support you. You would not like to live without a maid or a cook or your own carriage, would you? You are wasting your time on them, and possibly damaging your reputation in the process."

"I am doing no such thing!" cried Lydia. "It is only a little fun, Lizzy. Really, you ought not be so serious all the time."

"Let me make it clear to you, Lydia," said Elizabeth impatiently. "You look like a common trollop with your gown pulled so low you are practically spilling out of it."

Lydia gasped in offense but Elizabeth continued.

"The officers have no desire to wed you, though they likely wish to bed you and your behavior gives them reason to believe they will be successful. I would not be surprised to hear they are wagering on who will be the first to succeed!"

Lydia's eyes were as wide as her mouth now.

"Mr. Bingley is a respectable man with an independent fortune. If Jane is so lucky as to receive his addresses, he will be in a position to introduce his new sisters to his friends and take them to Town for a season. Do you think he will wish to introduce a loud, crass, drunk little girl in a London drawing room? Do you think your high spirits and lack of decorum will endear you to men of rank and wealth? Wake up, little sister. You have no dowry to speak of, no connections, and nothing but your youth to recommend you. Do not make it harder for yourself than it already is." Elizabeth took a deep breath, somewhat surprised at her own vehemence.

She finally looked at Lydia and saw her sister was so shocked she had not closed her mouth and was staring ahead of her blankly.

"I hardly think I am as bad as all that," said Lydia quietly. Her defense was all manufactured bravado and Elizabeth nearly relented and soothed her, but she thought it would be better for all to press her advantage.

"You are vain, ignorant, and idle," Elizabeth said in a softer voice.

Lydia looked away and bit her lip.

"But you do not have to be. You are not stupid, Lydia. You could make something of yourself if you wished to." Elizabeth pressed her arm and Lydia turned away sulkily, staring out the dark window. Elizabeth sighed and said, "I will leave you now. Please think on what I have said."

Lydia nodded but refused to look at her and Elizabeth thought it likely she was crying and did not want anyone to see her. Elizabeth knew she had been harsh, but she also believed it had been necessary. If Lydia was not checked firmly and soon, she would be completely ungovernable before her sixteenth year, and who knew what trouble she would get into. Elizabeth left the library and closed the door quietly behind her.

The ball had gone on in their absence. Mr. Collins had not been able to locate Elizabeth for the first set and so had asked Miss Lucas to stand up with him. Charlotte seemed happy enough to be asked and Elizabeth could only shake her head at her practical friend's behavior.

Elizabeth danced the second set with Captain Carter and just before it ended, she saw Lydia steal back into the ballroom quietly, her gown tugged up a little higher. Elizabeth caught her sister's eye and smiled. Lydia turned her head away in offense and Elizabeth had to laugh. Lydia was angry at her, but she had listened. Elizabeth knew it could be so much worse.

Lydia was subdued—for her— the remainder of the evening, though she did dance nearly every set and appeared to enjoy herself immensely. Mrs. Bennet was mostly appropriate in her volume, and the few times she began to crow about her daughter's fortune too loudly, Elizabeth shot her a look and Mrs. Bennet quieted, albeit unhappily.

Mr. Darcy claimed her for the fourth as he always did, and she wondered if she should use her newfound talent for bluntness on him.

Deciding it could not hurt, and truly wishing to know the answer, she asked, "Are you intending to remain much longer in Hertfordshire, Mr. Darcy?"

He was silent for a few minutes, and the dance moved them apart and back together again before he spoke. "My plans are not yet fixed, Miss Elizabeth. I do not believe I will remain much longer in the country."

She watched his solemn expression and replied, "I suppose that would not be wise, would it?" Her voice was softer than she intended, and he looked surprised for a moment.

"No, it would not," he finally said in a low tone.

She gave him a sad smile, and when the dance ended, he bowed low over her hand and she squeezed his tightly. They shared a look of mutual understanding and he walked away, his back straight and stiff and his mien unyielding.

Elizabeth sighed and found her way to the terrace. She was not truly surprised. She had known for some time he wouldn't stay in the area long past the ball. She expected nothing from him, and he owed nothing to her. But… he had become a friend of sorts and she would be sad to see him go.

She returned to the ballroom and accepted a request for the next dance. She went through the motions with little thought or enjoyment and was easily led to the dining room for supper. Jane requested she sit with her and Bingley and Elizabeth sat mechanically, realizing belatedly that she should have paid more attention to her chair's placement. She was seated right next to Caroline Bingley, and that lady did not look pleased by it. Elizabeth chose to ignore her upset and conversed with Jane until she heard Miss Bingley calling across the table to her brother.

"Where is Mr. Darcy, Charles? I haven't seen him in some time."

"I think he went to bed, Caroline. Said something about a headache," Bingley replied blithely. He went back to talking to Jane and Caroline huffed.

"Did he say anything else? Leave any message?" asked Caroline, clearly put out. "Perhaps he needs something."

Bingley was absorbed in his conversation with Jane and not paying his sister, or anyone, any attention.

Not getting the answer she wanted, Caroline began to rise from her seat when Elizabeth made a sound resembling a snort. Caroline looked at her through narrowed eyes.

"Does something amuse you, Miss Eliza?"

"You do," said Elizabeth, her good humor restored. And by Miss Bingley of all people!

"Me?" Caroline was incredulous and curious at the same time. "What have I done that is so amusing?"

"Your relentless pursuit of a man who has no interest in you whatsoever is quite amusing, Miss Bingley." She tilted her head to the side slightly. "Though it is also sad, in a way. I'm sure someone somewhere would appreciate what you have to offer. It is a pity Mr. Darcy does not."

Caroline flushed more deeply than anyone Elizabeth had ever seen. She would have felt sorry for her actions if Caroline was not also shooting daggers at her with her eyes.

"How dare you!" Caroline said in a low voice, filled with venom.

"I speak nothing but the truth, Miss Bingley. I know it is hard to hear sometimes, but there it is."

Caroline huffed. "You know nothing! How dare you say such things to me!"

"How dare you hound a man who is simply trying to enjoy his friend's company and a little hunting in the country!"

Caroline gasped and leaned closer. "I do not hound him," she whispered furiously. "I see to his needs, like a good hostess. Something *you* would know nothing about."

Elizabeth made no effort to hide how her eyes rolled at that statement. "Mr. Darcy has given you no encouragement and shown you no attention above that of his hostess and his close friend's sister. Has he ever given you reason, true reason, to believe he intends to offer for you?"

Caroline's jaw clenched.

"Or have you simply been hoping to wear him down? If that is your plan, I believe you are doomed to failure. Mr. Darcy is not one to tire easily, and if he finds himself annoyed by his company, he may simply leave. He is his own man. If you believe he will come to appreciate your qualities, you are deluding yourself. How long have you known him? How often have you been in company? If he wanted you, he would have proposed by now. He has not, so he must not desire your company for the remainder of his life."

The last bit had perhaps been a bit harsh, but really, Elizabeth had been talked down to, insulted, ignored, and treated shabbily by this woman from almost the first moment of their acquaintance. Caroline deserved whatever she got.

"You scheming little chit!" Caroline hissed. "Who are you? What do your opinions matter to me? You know nothing of Town, or the ton, or fashionable society." She flicked the lace on the sleeve of Elizabeth's best gown and sniffed. "As if the opinion of a Bennet matters to anyone. You are as ridiculous as your mother."

She might have left peacefully had Caroline not compared her to her mother. "At least I do not throw myself at men who do not desire my company. I may be a girl from the country, but the name Bennet has long been a proud one in Hertfordshire. We have held our estate for seven generations. Can you say the same?"

Caroline flushed again and sneered at Elizabeth.

"My mother may be ridiculous at times, but she loves her children and wants the best for them. Do you want the best for your brother? Or are all your machinations for your own selfish gain?"

Caroline sneered and finally said, "*You* question *me*? About my family?" Her affront knew no bounds and her indignation could not be contained.

Elizabeth stood and grasped the back of her chair with both hands. "I am a gentleman's daughter from a long line of landed gentlemen. You know what they say, Miss Bingley," she looked down her nose like a practiced society matron and spoke deliberately, "blood will out."

She turned on her heel and left the dining room. In a matter of minutes, she had gathered her cloak, asked a footman to inform her father she was leaving, and set off for Longbourn in the moonlight. She did not notice the tall man watching her leave from an upper window, nor did she notice the hot tears spilling down her cheeks.

Chapter 13

One Last Try

The next day was Tuesday once again, but Elizabeth couldn't bring herself to care. She went through her morning ablutions with a heavy heart, though she couldn't really say why. She thought it was distress at her many quarrels the day before, or exhaustion from the late night. It could be fatigue from this entire ordeal, living the same experiences day after day after day. She had many reasons to feel anxious and tired. But she knew in her heart it was none of these things.

No, her distress was wrapped up in a tall man from Derbyshire, and his unerring sense of duty that would not allow him to court her, or even call on her; he certainly would never offer for her. Somehow, knowing that he wished to, that if the decision was merely his and he had no family name to consider, no sister in his care, no grand estate to plan for, made it more painful.

She would not want a man who shirked his duty. She would not want a man who cared little for his own family or thought nothing of how his decisions affected them. It would have been so much easier to think him a coward and hate him for it. She couldn't even be properly angry with him.

She could not agree that their alliance would be so very bad, but she could respect his wish to honor his family name, and his desire to not hurt her by raising expectations he could not fulfill.

If only she had a proper dowry! Or at least one important relation on whose name she might trade. But she did not. She was Elizabeth Bennet of Longbourn, a small estate in Hertfordshire. Nothing more, and nothing less.

~

She could not continue like this. Her heart was a little more wounded each time she danced with him, each time she drew out that almost smile. She was so very happy at the thought of seeing him again, and so very sad when she remembered that *he* did not come to each ball with the memory of their past dances and conversations. He did not feel a little closer to her each time they danced or conversed.

She could not take this anymore! Something must be done! She had no idea why she was repeating the same day incessantly, but she could not simply sit back and allow her life to be taken over by some horrible curse. She must act.

She had stopped her family from embarrassing themselves, encouraged Bingley to propose, worked on Mr. Darcy and Miss Bingley. None of it had worked.

But... she had never tried all of her plans together. Armed with the most intricate plan of all, Elizabeth set to work.

Her first stop was Jane's room, where she encouraged her sister to encourage Mr. Bingley. She knew Jane would need to be told multiple times and in a variety of ways throughout the day, so Elizabeth started early. Then she went to Mary. Her next youngest sister was given sheet music for the evening, unsolicited advice for her attire, and an offer to help with her hair.

Elizabeth next made her way to the stillroom with a bottle of laudanum, then asked Lydia to try the mulberry wine she had made. (She was in no mood to try another attack on the stairs.) Once Lydia was safely ensconced in her bed, Elizabeth took tea to her mother, and brought the bottle of wine just in case. Soon Mrs. Bennet was sleeping peacefully and Elizabeth stopped by Jane's room to give her another round of reassurance. She was already feeling fatigue from her exertions, but at the same time she felt an undercurrent of energy.

Her plan just might work.

When she arrived at the ball—and survived her awful dance with Mr. Collins (that was one event that never improved with experience), she did everything in her power to convince Miss Bingley not to leave Hertfordshire. She complimented her looks, scared her with stories of disease in London, and hinted that her intimacy with Mr. Darcy was greatly increased while they resided in the same house. She left Miss Bingley looking thoughtful and sought out Mr. Bingley for a set.

They were halfway through the dance when she boldly asked, "Are you a good brother, Mr. Bingley?" He looked at her with confusion and she continued, "I would like to know what I am getting into." She smiled slyly and he flushed crimson and looked at Jane.

She would have thought herself too bold but for her knowledge that he truly did care for her sister and only wanted a little nudge to propose. She saw the moment he gathered his courage and decided to speak.

"Yes, I believe I am a good brother, but Louisa and Caroline would probably be better judges of that."

She thought differently, but she kept that to herself. "I am glad to hear it." The dance separated them for a moment and when she returned to him she said, "Am I to gain such a good brother soon, do you think?"

He was clearly shocked by her audacity, but Elizabeth was well past the point of caring whom she shocked anymore.

When his face returned to its usual color, he said, "I imagine it will be soon, Miss Elizabeth. I see no reason to delay."

She smiled brightly at him. "I am so very glad to hear that, Mr. Bingley. I am certain my sister will be, too."

"Truly? You believe she is ready to," he fumbled for words and turned about in the dance, then returned to her looking flustered but determined. "It is your belief that Jane is ready to receive my proposals?"

"She is ready and eager, Mr. Bingley. You need have no concerns on that count."

He smiled so brightly she could count all his teeth and skipped through the movements like a colt in spring. She could not restrain her laughter and he joined her, spinning her about a bit too strongly, but they were both too happy to truly mind.

"Soon I shall claim a brother's privilege and call you Lizzy," he said, proud as a peacock.

"I would like that. Shall I then call you Charlie?"

He made a face and she laughed at it, prompting him to smile and say, "You may if you wish. Louisa called me Charlie when I was a boy, as did my mother, but no one has done so in many years."

She thought she saw sadness behind the brightness in his eyes and her heart went out to him. The dance ended and as she rose from her curtsy she said, "Then I shall look forward to a sister's privilege. Now go claim Jane before someone else does!"

He practically ran across the room and took her sister's hand, whispering in Jane's ear. Soon they were walking out to the garden and Elizabeth was sighing with relief. So far, all was going according to plan.

"Is Mr. Bingley going to propose, do you think?" asked Charlotte.

Elizabeth smiled. "He is. He as much as told me so during our dance."

"Truly?" Charlotte looked impressed.

"They will be very happy together, I think."

"Yes, I think they are well-suited. Your mother will be pleased."

Elizabeth groaned. "Do not remind me of what is to come. I was having such a lovely evening."

Charlotte laughed at her friend. "What mother wouldn't be happy at seeing a daughter so well settled? And if Mr. Collins marries one of her daughters, her home will be secured for her lifetime."

"I do not think that will happen," said Elizabeth firmly.

"You intend to refuse him then?" asked Charlotte.

Elizabeth whipped her head to look at her friend. She supposed she shouldn't be surprised Charlotte had noticed her cousin's dogged pursuit of her. "Yes, I do. He would make me miserable, and I am certain I would make him so. I don't know what Mama was thinking when she pushed him towards me."

"She was thinking Jane would make a match with Mr. Bingley and you were the next eldest. Not to mention the prettiest of the remaining sisters."

"How neatly you qualify remaining sisters," she teased. "I know I am not as pretty as Jane—"

"No one is as pretty as Jane," interrupted Charlotte.

Elizabeth nodded in agreement. "But Kitty is quite pretty, and Mary is more attractive when she makes an effort. Besides, I believe Mama put me forward because I am her least favorite, not because of my seniority. She did not want to waste one of her favorites on Mr. Collins."

Charlotte made a face. "You may be right. Your mother's tastes have always been suspect."

Elizabeth laughed. "What a true friend you are! How shall I repay you for such a lovely compliment?"

"Convince Mr. Darcy to dance with me. My mother will not be

able to stop crowing of it and it will bring me no end of amusement."

Elizabeth laughed. "Very well, my friend, I will do it if it can be done."

Charlotte looked over her friend's shoulder. "Good, because I believe Mr. Darcy is coming over to ask you to dance."

After sharing a mischievous look with Charlotte, Elizabeth turned and smiled brightly at Mr. Darcy. She accepted his request for the next set and Charlotte would have teased her mercilessly for it had Jane not come rushing over to tell them about her engagement to Charles Bingley. Bingley had gone straight to Mr. Bennet to ask for his blessing and an audience the next morning. Elizabeth was truly happy for her sister, and when Mr. Darcy collected her for their dance, she was positively glowing.

"Is it not a lovely evening, Mr. Darcy?" she asked dreamily, floating on the happy cloud of her success and her sister's happiness.

"Yes, quite."

"Come now, Mr. Darcy! You can do better than that! The moon is bright, the stars are shining, the music is lively, and your partner is light of foot. Could anything improve this night?"

He smiled at her joy and said, "You are quite right, Miss Elizabeth. There is everything to be pleased with tonight."

"That's much better. Now what shall we talk about?"

The left side of his mouth quirked up again in the half smile she had come to know so well. "Tell me what you would most like to hear and I will endeavor to oblige you."

She shook her head and said, "Tell me about Pemberley." His surprise was obvious so she helped him along. "Does it have a large wood?"

"Yes, the woods are extensive."

"Are there riding or walking trails throughout? What manner of wildlife live in it? Is there a brook or river you fish in?"

His half-smile appeared again and she looked at him expectantly. "Very well, Miss Elizabeth. I see what you are after. There is a brook of a decent size, and a few smaller streams, and most of them run into the larger river on the east side of the estate."

He continued talking, telling her about the deer and the birds and the seasons of the Peak District. She asked about the river and the lake he told her stood near the house. He spoke of his favorite place to fish and she agreed it sounded lovely. He gave her an overview of the entire estate, from the house to the home farm to the hunting lodge, and she asked intelligent questions and remained interested throughout their two dances. She had never heard him speak with such ease or at such length, and both were a little surprised when the music stopped and the other dancers began bowing to their partners.

"Thank you for the dance, Mr. Darcy. It was delightful."

"The pleasure was mine, Miss Elizabeth." He bowed very correctly.

"I wonder if I might ask a favor of you?"

"What can I do for you?"

"My dearest friend, Charlotte Lucas, has not had many partners tonight. Would you be so kind as to ask her to dance?" When she saw his serious expression she added hastily, "She is an excellent dancer, sir, and her conversation is well informed." She smiled beguilingly and felt a moment of triumph when she saw his shoulders relax slightly and his resolve give way.

"Very well. I shall ask her."

She beamed at him. "Thank you, Mr. Darcy. It is kind of you."

Elizabeth had a very pleasant ball after that. Her mother and Lydia were not there to embarrass her, Mary played a simple—and blessedly short—song at supper, and her father announced Jane's engagement. Elizabeth thought he made the announcement partially to aggravate her mother. Mrs. Bennet would be terribly put out when she found out she had missed not only the most important ball of the season, but her own daughter's engagement. Elizabeth chose not to worry about it. She would never be able to change her parents, and it would be futile to try. But she would remember to keep laudanum on hand in future.

Finally, the ball came to a close. Elizabeth happily fetched her cloak and was about to wrap it about her when it was taken from her hands. She looked up into the dark eyes of Mr. Darcy.

"Allow me, Miss Elizabeth."

She nodded silently and he wrapped the cloak around her shoulders with the utmost care. He fastened the button at the top and his hands lingered there for just a moment until Elizabeth broke the silence.

"I would like some fresh air. Will you escort me?"

"Of course."

He led her out the front door and down the steps, out of the way of the drive where carriages were being pulled up and loaded with passengers. They stepped off the gravel into the grass where the house receded, falling into the shadow of the grand structure.

Elizabeth took a deep breath and looked up at the stars, then to Mr. Darcy.

"Thank you for dancing with Charlotte. That was kind of you."

"You need not thank me. It is the duty of gentlemen at balls."

She swallowed her laugh and looked at his profile. He really was terribly handsome. "Jane also enjoyed her dance with you."

"She is to marry my friend," he said by way of explanation.

She smiled. He was so very proud, and so very sure of being right, but she did not find it as off putting as she once had. She would almost call it endearing now. In essentials, he was a very good sort of man. He was wanting in liveliness and manners, but the right person might bring out a lighter side to him, and his manners could improve with time.

She ceased her musing long enough to notice Mr. Darcy staring at her, his dark eyes fixed on hers.

"Forgive me, sir, I was woolgathering."

"May I ask to where your thoughts roamed?"

She flushed. "I do not think that would interest you, Mr. Darcy."

"Oh?"

She wondered how he could disarm her with one tiny word.

"I wonder if the weather will hold," he said finally.

"I do not know. It would make your trip to Town easier if it were fine."

He looked at her in some surprise and she said, "Come now, Mr. Darcy. It is obvious you wish to leave Hertfordshire as soon as possible. I imagine you only stayed as long as you did for the ball." She tried to keep her tone light but she suspected she failed rather dreadfully.

He looked at her, his heart in his eyes, and said, "Would that I could stay, Miss Elizabeth."

She swallowed and nodded shakily. "I know. You must do your duty. Don't worry, Mr. Darcy. I understand." She looked down and back up swiftly. "I will not hold it against you."

He looked at her sadly and gifted her with one of his rare smiles. "I have very much enjoyed making your acquaintance, Miss Bennet."

"And I yours, Mr. Darcy."

They stared at each other silently for a painfully long moment. Somehow his hand found its way to hers and squeezed her fingers tightly.

"I shall never see you again, shall I?" she asked softly.

He swallowed thickly and took a shaky breath, unable to speak.

Knowing it may be her last chance to do so, she reached up and touched his face. She traced her fingers along his jaw, and her hand cupped his cheek. She lifted onto her toes and kissed his face, just to the side of his mouth, close enough to feel his breath hitch, and lingered there for a moment before lowering her heels, removing her hand, and stepping away from him.

She watched him silently, green eyes meeting brown. He looked utterly stricken, as if he had lost someone very dear to him, and she felt the compliment of his affection, unspoken though it was.

"Goodbye, Mr. Darcy."

He bowed deeply, and she turned and ran before he had straightened.

Chapter 14

To Know Herself

Elizabeth awoke the next morning not caring what day it was. Tuesday, Wednesday, what difference did it make? Mr. Darcy would leave regardless, and she would be alone, and they would never know what might have been. Jane would marry Bingley and she would remain at Longbourn, alone, forever. She put her pillow over her head and went back to sleep.

She eventually woke and prepared for the day. Why had she tried so hard to fix things? Clearly, focusing on enjoying herself at the ball had been a better plan than anything else she had tried. She was tired of trying to fix Jane's life, fix Lydia's behavior, fix Mary's manners, fix her father's indolence, fix her mother's vulgarity. It was exhausting! Why could she not fix her own life? She had done everything in her power to take care of everyone else, and in some ways, she had been successful. Her mother had been nearly quiet for an entire evening, Lydia had actually appeared thoughtful, and Mr. Bingley had proposed to Jane twice. Really, she was very good at arranging things. If only fate would recognize her talents and let her be!

Feeling a sudden urge to walk, she put on her half boots and made for the garden. In her angry swishing of a long twig, she accidentally knocked the blossom off the last remaining dahlia, its bright petals falling to the ground in a pink swirl. She was so frustrated she wanted to cry. Was life not difficult enough? She had to compound it by destroying the only flower left in the entire garden? She sat down on the nearest bench and wept from sheer exhaustion.

Finally, after a good cry and feeling thoroughly sorry for herself, she knew it was time to face the true source of her distress: her affection for Mr. Darcy.

She knew not why it took her so long to understand her own

feelings, nor why she had had such a difficult time accepting them. Perhaps it was because Mr. Darcy had called her tolerable and not handsome enough, or perhaps it was because she took a perverse pride in seeing how well she tempted him after all. Regardless, she was now in a wretched state, for she held Mr. Darcy very dear, and she was sure she would call it love if she but let herself believe it to be possible. She knew he held her in similar affection, but his duty was to marry wealth and connections, and she brought neither. Regardless of how he felt for her, he would not offer for her. It was best to try to forget him and move forward with her life.

If only doing what was best did not make her feel so very wretched.

Elizabeth prepared for that night's ball with no agenda. She would dance, she would have a good time, but she would not try to accomplish anything. It never worked, anyhow. She went through all the usual motions of greeting the hosts and saying hello to her friends. She danced the first with Mr. Collins and the second with Captain Carter. The third she sat out to talk to Charlotte. Mr. Darcy requested the fourth, as she knew he would.

She accepted, though she had been tempted to refuse. It was so disheartening, standing across from the man one wished one had an understanding with, night after night, with nary a reprieve. She nearly laughed at the irony. She hoped for a future with him, one where they might live together and see each other every day. Did she not see him every day as it was? A nearly hysterical laugh escaped her.

Mr. Darcy quirked an eyebrow, but he was too much a gentleman to call out her odd behavior. He was gallant and polite, and they danced quietly. Afterward, he offered to get her some punch. She thanked him, and they stood side by side sipping their drinks, watching the partygoers.

"Are you well, Miss Elizabeth?" he asked quietly.

She turned to face him but made no answer.

"You do not seem yourself this evening," he added softly.

She sighed and fought the urge to begin cackling hysterically in the middle of the ballroom. "I am well in body, though slightly worn in spirits. Thank you for asking."

"Is there anything I may do for you?"

It was terribly unfair that his voice should be so exactly pitched to bring her comfort and inspire trust.

"I do not believe there is, though I would like to get out of this room. It is stuffy," she said.

He immediately took her by the elbow and led her out of the ballroom, across the hall and down a small corridor that she knew led to the library.

"You will not be disturbed here."

He led her to the sofa by the window and she thanked him for his thoughtfulness. He seemed as if he had something to say to her but could not make himself say the words. Or perhaps she was imagining things.

He shifted his weight from one foot to the other, then said, "May I bring you anything?"

"No, I am quite well."

After several more rather painful minutes passed in awkwardness, she broke the silence. "Is there something on your mind, Mr. Darcy?"

He looked startled at the sound of her voice. "Yes. No. That is, I wanted to tell you Miss Elizabeth, that I have quite enjoyed making your acquaintance."

"As I have enjoyed coming to know you."

He looked at her oddly. "Thank you. I am very glad we met."

"As am I." She smiled in a reassuring manner. "Goodbye, Mr. Darcy."

He seemed surprised that she understood his intentions, and then relieved. "Goodbye, my dear Miss Elizabeth."

He bowed, she nodded, and he left. She waited until she heard his footsteps receding down the corridor and then she leapt up and began to pace the length of the room.

Oh, how tempted she had been! She had wanted to ask him to pretend there was no tomorrow, to live today as if it were their last day on earth, to have no secrets from each other, to bare their hearts. But she could not. All this stress was making her dramatic. She was sure that she never would have considered such a thing a month ago. Was it the repetition causing the change in her character or the ball itself? If the ball was to blame, that would explain why women who were overly social were also somewhat histrionic.

Shaking off the ridiculous idea, she returned her thoughts to the issue at hand: how she was to get through this and additional balls without saying something embarrassingly inappropriate to Mr. Darcy, or worse, throwing herself into his arms like a pathetic heroine in a melodramatic novel. She knew it was silly, but she desperately wanted to hear him say how he felt about her. She had seen it in his eyes, and felt his fingers squeeze her hand, and he had shown her in a dozen little ways, but she wanted to hear the words. An admission of affection, of love, of attraction even. She wanted something!

It would be such a relief to hear it, and another to unburden her own heart. She longed to tell him how her opinion of him had changed, and how sorry she was for doubting his goodness for so long. She wanted to beg him not to forget her too quickly.

She bit her lip and looked about the dark library, feeling all the ridiculousness of her position. "Stop mooning about, Lizzy! That's enough now," she scolded herself.

Her eyes lit on a small writing desk against the far wall and suddenly, she had an idea.

~

It had taken her more than an hour, but she had finally written a letter she was mostly happy with. Now to deliver it. She made it upstairs to the family wing without being seen, but she was not sure which bedroom was Mr. Darcy's. She only knew he was on this corridor because she had seen him leaving it when she stayed at Netherfield nursing Jane.

She crept to the first door and listened for movement. It would be disastrous to walk in on a servant turning down the bed. She knew the room to her left was Louisa's. She imagined the room next to it, or possibly across from it, belonged to Mr. Hurst. She would be very surprised if they shared a room. She opened the door across the hall and looked inside. It was dark and still, with only a little light shining in from the window. She had only gone a few steps when she realized she was in Caroline Bingley's room. She could smell her perfume quite clearly.

She resisted the urge to play some sort of joke on Caroline (if she'd had a frog handy, she couldn't honestly say she wouldn't have put it in Miss Bingley's bed), and left the room as quietly as she'd come in. She tried the room next to it. She thought it would be like Miss Bingley to place Darcy so near herself, but surely her brother and Mrs. Hurst would have objected. The rooms were designed enfilade, each room connecting to the one next to it. Miss Bingley was a bit desperate, but

Elizabeth didn't think she would put herself in a situation that may call her reputation into question.

Sure enough, the next room belonged to Mr. Bingley. She recognized his walking stick in the corner, and it didn't smell like Mr. Darcy. The one across the hall she thought likely to be Mr. Hurst's as it was next to Louisa's, so she skipped it. There were two rooms remaining at the end of the hall with a window between them, thankfully adding some light to the corridor. She looked out the window and thought the better view would be the room on her right, next to Mr. Bingley's. Surely Caroline would have insisted Darcy have the best room. She listened carefully at the door, and hearing nothing, she opened it slowly.

A few steps into the room and she knew she had guessed correctly. Whatever scent Mr. Darcy used was present here, though not nearly as strongly as Caroline's perfume had been in her room. There was a small writing table in the corner, and on it a traveling desk set. Perfect! She would place her letter on it and—she stopped. He would not look at his desk set before he went to bed, and the letter would be gone in the morning along with all memory of today. She turned and saw the grand bed with its damask cover and heavy curtains. She would have to place the letter there, on his pillow, to be certain he found it before he went to sleep.

She approached the bed slowly, mindful of creaking floorboards and the fact that she was alone in a man's bedroom for the first time in her entire life. If she were caught here, her reputation would be in tatters. For the rest of the night anyway. Elizabeth huffed. The bed was not yet turned down. His valet would come to turn down the bed, see the letter, and her plan would be in jeopardy. She had no idea what the valet would do with it. He might put it with Darcy's other correspondence. He might simply hand it to his master or put it back where he found it. He could think it was from Caroline, due to its location and mode of delivery, and throw it in the fire or not give it to Darcy for days or even weeks!

Her imagination was clearly too accustomed to designing grand schemes to think clearly. She took a deep breath and shook off her silliness. The way forward was clear. She would turn down the bed herself. The valet would come in to do it and think the 'tween stairs maid had done it. If the maid usually did it, she would think the valet had done it. It was unlikely anyone would raise a fuss over someone else doing their job. Once she had the coverlet and linen turned down and sufficiently straight, she fluffed the pillows up and laid them flat on the bed. Which pillow did he sleep on? She thought to put the letter under the pillow to avoid someone else finding it and disposing of it, but he might not find it there.

Finally, she decided to place it vertically between the two pillows. It was fairly likely the person in the bed would notice it, but not a person who just gave the bed a cursory glance. She stood back and looked at the arrangement and thought it was as good as she could do under the circumstances. Satisfied she had accomplished her mission, she crept back out of the room and down the corridor to the stairs, then back to the ballroom.

There was only one dance left. She cajoled her father into dancing it with her, and she ended the evening laughing with the one who had taught her to laugh at herself—and everyone else—and not to take life too seriously. He had his faults, but she loved her father dearly. It was the perfect way to end the night.

She caught Mr. Darcy watching them from the side with an odd expression on his face, and she could not help nodding his direction with a sweet smile. When her father teased her about smiling at Mr. Darcy just because he had finally decided to dance with her, she was able to reply honestly, "He is amiable Father, truly. You do not know him. Let us not judge before we know him as more than a passing acquaintance."

Mr. Bennet raised his brows. "Very well, Lizzy. I bow to your superior judgment," he teased. Lord love him, but her father would never change.

~

The next morning Elizabeth woke so early the sun was barely shining through the slit in the curtains. Pleased to have some time to herself, she dressed quickly and slipped out for a walk, a hot muffin pilfered from the kitchen in her pocket. She went halfway to Oakham Mount before turning back. She would have liked to go farther, but her mother would rise soon and wonder where she was.

She couldn't stop thinking of the letter she had written to Mr. Darcy. She knew it by heart, having written several versions before deciding on the one she would deliver. She recited it in her mind, wondering if he had found it, and what he had thought when he read it.

Was he scandalized? Horrified? Flattered? Frightened?

She would never know, but she had felt better for writing it, and better still for delivering it to his keeping. It felt right somehow for him to know how she felt. She couldn't explain it, she simply felt how very important it had been to unburden herself, to tell him of her heart. She smiled when she thought of it.

Dear Mr. Darcy,

Please forgive my impropriety in writing this letter, but I could not bring myself to say the words to you in person. I know this will make little sense to you, and indeed, you may even now be wondering if I am a little mad, but I simply must tell you.

You have become very dear to me. As a valued friend, as a pleasant dance partner, and as a man. I am sorry that circumstances are such that we will never be able to deepen our friendship or discover if this attraction between us could lead to something more fulfilling.

You will leave Hertfordshire soon, and I will likely never see you again. I must ask you to do something for me. As you are an honorable gentleman, I know you will consider my request seriously, and I pray you will take it to heart.

Please be careful, my friend. Do not get caught up in some matron's schemes, or bow to the pressure of society or even your family. You are a good man, a worthy man, and you deserve a wife who will appreciate and value you, not one who simply wishes to add your family name and estate to her list of recent acquisitions. Guard your heart—protect it fiercely—as I would do if I had the privilege.

You will live long in my memory as the first gentleman of my acquaintance. It has been an honor getting to know you these past weeks. I am touched that you have shared as much of yourself with me as you have. I know this makes little sense to you—please do not try to understand it, for it cannot be understood. I doubt you will even recall this letter in the morning. Put it from your mind.

Suffice it to say that I am honored by your trust and bewildered and honored again by your affection. It is not unrequited.

Take care, my dear Mr. Darcy. May God bless you.

Your Elizabeth

She sighed. It was far from perfect, but it had been honest, and that was what she most wanted it to be. It little mattered, anyhow. She would see him again at the ball tonight and it would be as if it never happened, as if their conversations and looks and stolen touches were all in her imagination.

She had made it back to the garden near the house now. She looked around at the dormant rose bushes and wondered if she would ever see them in bloom again. She walked past the bare dahlias and made her way toward the back door. She stopped. She turned slowly, an eerie feeling creeping over her. She stole back toward the flower bed and looked at the dahlias. They were a hardy flower, always blooming into late autumn, occasionally into early winter. She had noticed a late-blooming dahlia nearly every day of the curse. The stems were bare now. She looked to the ground, and there were the pink petals she had knocked over yesterday, still strewn at her feet.

She stared in shock for a few moments, then turned and ran into the house like her boots were on fire. She burst into the kitchen, startling a maid into dropping a bowl on the stone floor.

"What day is it?" Elizabeth cried. Two maids and Cook looked at her as if she were deranged.

"What day is it?" she cried again.

"It is Wednesday, Miss. The twenty-seventh of November," said Cook.

"Wednesday?" Elizabeth thought she might faint. Wednesday! And she had not stayed up all night, or convinced Mr. Bingley to propose to Jane, or drugged her mother with laudanum. How could this be?

Cook led her to sit at the table and brought her a cup of tea and set a small plate of food in front of her.

"Eat something, Miss Lizzy. It helps," said Cook.

Elizabeth laughed. It began as a small chortle only she could hear, then it was a giggle, then she was laughing so loudly the staff was worried for her sanity. Finally, she thanked Cook kindly and took the tea and food to her room where she might mentally unravel without an audience.

Of all the days for time to revert back to normal, it would be the one in which she had written a letter she had no chance of getting back.

Chapter 15

In Which Elizabeth Tempts Fate

Her family began to wake one by one, and Elizabeth knew what she had to do. She knocked on her mother's door and stepped inside.

"May I have a word, Mama?"

"What is it, Lizzy?"

"Mr. Collins will ask for a private audience today."

Mrs. Bennet's face lit up. "I knew it! We are saved!"

Elizabeth grabbed her mother's hands before they took flight and interrupted her exclamations. "Mother, I need you to listen very carefully to me. Will you do that?"

Mrs. Bennet huffed and looked displeased but agreed to listen.

"Mr. Collins and I will not suit." She held her hand up when her mother tried to protest. "We would make each other miserable, and while I am well aware of the advantages of the match, they are not enough for me to sacrifice my entire life. You do not truly want me to be mistress of Longbourn, Mama. In your heart you know you do not wish to live with me all your days."

Mrs. Bennet grumbled, "I might if you were more agreeable and not so apt to run on as you do."

Elizabeth smiled in resignation. "I know you will be terribly disappointed if I refuse him, so I am suggesting an alternative."

Mrs. Bennet was sulking with her arms crossed, looking every bit the petulant child. She looked at her least favorite daughter warily. "What alternative?"

"Deny him an audience. Do whatever you can to put him off and encourage him towards one of your other daughters. Though I would not wish such a ridiculous man on anyone, he has no malice in him. Might he do for Mary or Kitty?" Mrs. Bennet looked thoughtful and

Elizabeth drove the point home. "He will not stay and seek another Bennet bride if I refuse him. And I *will* refuse him, Mama."

Mrs. Bennet was considering the idea, but she did not wish to give her plans up so easily. After all, she was still the mistress of Longbourn and the mother of this impertinent young lady. "You ought to do your duty to your family. Your father has let you have your own way too often, and now you don't—"

Elizabeth interrupted her. "My father will support me in this. I know he will. Even if he did not, you do not want me to be mistress of this house, Mama. I would immediately cut your allowance to a pittance and begin work on the dower house."

Mrs. Bennet gasped. "You wouldn't!"

"I would." Elizabeth stared at her mother with eyes like flint and Mrs. Bennet leaned back.

"Perhaps he would do for Mary," she said quietly.

Elizabeth nodded. "Now, to make matters easier, I shall go for a long walk and visit Charlotte at Lucas Lodge. That should be enough time for you to tell Mr. Collins that his interest in me has been misplaced. Tell him I am in love with another, tell him an old friend has come to seek my hand and has a prior claim, tell him one of your other daughters is in love with him and it would be too cruel for me to marry him. It does not matter to me so long as you tell him *privately* and he understands that his pursuit of me will not end happily."

Mrs. Bennet nodded. "I will tell him you have long been in love with Arthur Goulding. He is returning home from his grand tour and you hope for a match."

"Remember to tell him privately and quietly, Mama. I don't want rumors spread. And better to simply say 'a young man' and leave Mr. Goulding's name out of it."

Mrs. Bennet nodded, her mind already on the conversation she was to have with Collins.

"And Mama?"

"Yes?"

"Mary is quite pretty when she takes a little time with her appearance. She is not so dull as everyone thinks she is. You might privately talk to her, or better yet, offer to arrange her hair. She is open to suggestions if they are given kindly."

Mrs. Bennet nodded, the scheming glint Elizabeth was well

familiar with in her eyes. Elizabeth shook her head. It was out of her hands now. She had rid herself of Mr. Collins. Now she had other affairs to see to.

~

Elizabeth spent the day discussing the ball with Charlotte and returned home with only enough time to change for dinner. Mr. Collins was easily avoided during that meal, and she saw him looking between her and Mary with a thoughtful expression she chose to believe was a good sign.

She knew the Netherfield party would leave the following day, but she was unsure how to stop them from going. She thought it unlikely she could truly accomplish anything and chose instead to focus her energy on supporting Jane.

She walked into Meryton Thursday with her sisters and ran into Mr. Wickham and Mr. Denny. Kitty blushed as she spoke to Denny and Elizabeth decided to have a conversation with her father about it. It might not do much good, but she hadn't lost all hope for him yet. Lydia was brazen and overly flirtatious, as expected. Elizabeth thought a repeat of her harsh lecture might be in order.

Mr. Wickham sidled up to her, all easy smiles and smooth charm.

"Did you enjoy the ball, Miss Elizabeth?"

She valiantly kept her eyes from rolling. "It was a lovely evening, Mr. Wickham. Did you enjoy your sojourn in London?"

"Town was everything it always is. I am sorry to have missed the ball, of course. I had very much looked forward to dancing with you," he said with a smile.

Had she truly thought him charming? He was all artifice and empty compliments. "Then I am surprised you did not simply attend the ball. I understood Mr. Bingley issued an invitation to all the officers."

He was momentarily surprised by her tone but was soon back to amiable civility. "I thought it best to avoid Mr. Darcy while he is in the area. I did not wish to upset Mr. Bingley's gathering with an unpleasant scene."

"If you are so intent on avoiding Mr. Darcy, and not damaging the son's name for the sake of the father's memory, I wonder why you speak of him so frequently. If you truly wished to start anew, you could have ignored him and never said a word. Mr. Darcy certainly has not sought you out nor slandered your name in any way." She kept her tone light and tilted her head to one side, as if she were considering a puzzle. "It is curious."

He shifted uncomfortably. "Miss Bennet, forgive me if my confidence has upset you or made your interactions with Mr. Darcy unpleasant. That was not my intention."

"Truly? Hmm." It was clear from her expression that she did not believe him. "A word of advice, if I may, Mr. Wickham. If you wish to gain sympathy from the local populace, do not do it with stories easily disproved and words designed to malign and misconstrue. One might wonder why you needed sympathy at all," she said evenly.

His shock was evident, and his wide eyes held a spark of fear.

"Peddle your poison elsewhere, Mr. Wickham. It is not welcome here." She gave him one final stare and turned to go home, taking her sisters with her.

Once back at Longbourn, she decided to have a talk with her father. It was long overdue and she found she had greater courage after her ordeal. Some things were worth the discomfort of an awkward conversation. Her family's respectability was one of them.

Her father invited her to sit and rang for tea. Elizabeth prepared his cup the way he liked it and mentally steeled herself for what she must tell him. She began with the tale of Mr. Wickham and how he was spreading falsehoods about Mr. Darcy. His audience had thus far been limited, but she would not be surprised if he told it to all and sundry when Mr. Darcy left the neighborhood.

Mr. Bennet, in his usual dry humor, asked what this had to do with him. This was the truly difficult part. She began to speak of Lydia's behavior, using evidence from the Netherfield ball, Meryton assemblies, and other events the family had attended. She described how her youngest sister uniformly flaunted convention and humiliated her family. Lydia was loud, crass, and vulgar. She was not fit for polite society and should not be out until she was.

Mr. Bennet was surprised by both her vehemence and the fact that she had brought this to him at all.

Elizabeth refused to stop. She went on about Lydia's inappropriate attire, and the things the officers said about her when they thought no one could hear them. Mr. Bennet flushed an angry red and Elizabeth thought maybe she was on the right track. She told him Lydia usually pulled her dresses down even lower after she had left the house and described in detail her sister's antics designed to gain the soldier's attention. Mr. Bennet was clearly uncomfortable, but Elizabeth would not stop.

"If you do not take the trouble to check her, she will become the most determined flirt to ever make herself and her family ridiculous."

Mr. Bennet made some noise about it not being as bad as that, and that she and Jane would be respected wherever they went. Elizabeth did not wish to hear it. She accused him of willful blindness, of hiding in his bookroom away from the realities of their life, content to let Mrs. Bennet, who clearly was not fit for the job, manage raising their daughters and launching them into society.

She thought he was really angry at this point, and she apologized for her harshness, but not for her words. Something must be done! If he loved his daughters at all, he must act. Their very respectability depended on it. And after all, what else did they have?

She rose to leave the room and stopped just before the door to deliver one parting shot.

"You cannot give us dowries, sir, but you can give us a name to be proud of."

He looked stricken and angry, and she hastily left, closing the door behind her.

~

Mr. Bennet avoided Elizabeth for the next three days. He took all his meals in his bookroom and when he passed her in a corridor, he pretended not to see her. She chose to view it as a positive reaction. If he had truly ignored her and everything she had said, he would not be so bothered by her presence. He must be giving her words at least some consideration.

Unbeknownst to Elizabeth, Mr. Bennet went into Meryton to collect an order from the bookstore. Elizabeth and Jane had accompanied Kitty and Lydia into town, and as he stepped out of the small shop, he saw his two youngest daughters running down the street towards a group of red coats, their elder sisters calling at them to slow down. Unsurprisingly, they were ignored.

He laughed at their antics, already knowing them to be very silly girls, but Elizabeth's words stayed in his mind. He looked at his girls from another point of view. He saw the town's people shaking their heads at them. He saw Elizabeth and Jane flushing in embarrassment. The officers watched the girls running towards them with expressions he was not altogether comfortable with.

With a deep sigh, and more than a little resentment at being forced to act at all, he marched across the street and ordered Kitty and Lydia into the carriage. They were not happy to go, but so shocked by his presence in Meryton that they complied quickly. Jane and Elizabeth looked relieved, and he gave them each a few coins to buy something for themselves while he took their sisters home.

That night, Mr. and Mrs. Bennet had the greatest row in the history of their marriage. Their daughters lined up on the stairs, listening silently and wondering what had brought it on. Mrs. Bennet had not closed the bookroom door entirely and the girls could hear most of what was said.

Mr. Bennet was furious that Jane and Elizabeth, two perfectly nice, well-behaved girls were being punished and embarrassed for the horrid behavior of their sisters. They could not even enjoy a simple outing because they were forced to watch over Kitty and Lydia like mother hens, lest the younger girls disgrace the family.

Jane and Elizabeth, side by side on the lowest step, looked at each other in shock. Was that truly their father speaking? Lydia huffed, as expected, and Kitty listened wide-eyed. Mary sat on the uppermost step, for eavesdropping was wrong and she could not condone it, but the top step presented a moral medium for her.

Mrs. Bennet defended her daughters, saying they were lively and fun loving, and such favorites with the officers. Mr. Bennet roared that that was the problem. They were the daughters of gentlemen, not shopkeepers' daughters there to entertain lowly militia men. He went on to say Kitty was not strongminded enough to be cavorting through town on her own, and Lydia was simply too young to be out at all.

Lydia made to protest at this and Elizabeth turned around and silenced her sister. If their parents found them there, the girls would not hear the remainder of the argument and they would be chastised besides. Lydia grumbled but closed her mouth.

In the end, their parents agreed that Lydia would not attend functions unless they were at Longbourn or at the homes of close friends. Kitty would be supervised more closely. No more walks into Meryton, no more tea with the officers. And absolutely no Mr.

Wickham. He was a liar, a gambler, and a seducer. Mr. Bennet would not have one of his daughters end up high in the belly because of that cur's smooth tongue.

The five girls on the stairs paled and Lydia looked truly shocked. It was at this point they decided to scurry upstairs to their rooms and wait for their father to call them and inform them of the new rules.

Mr. Bennet did so the next day, and though Kitty and Lydia were upset, Mr. Bennet quickly informed them that the more they bellyached and grumbled, the longer it would be before they gained their freedom. Lydia snapped her mouth shut, but she was not happy.

Elizabeth had never been more proud of her father.

Chapter 16

The Gentleman Returns

A week after the Netherfield ball, or more than a month after, depending on one's method of counting, Mr. Bingley appeared at Netherfield. Caroline had sent a note, three days after the ball, saying they were removing to Town for the winter and did not know when they would return. Jane had been upset, but as the note had not mentioned anything about Georgiana Darcy or any of their friends in Town, Jane had easily been calmed by Elizabeth who assured her sister that she knew, without a doubt, that Mr. Bingley loved her. Elizabeth's conviction was such that Jane could not deny her, and she had waited patiently for his return.

Mr. Bingley quickly made an appearance at Longbourn. Jane was as enamored as ever, and Mrs. Bennet was beside herself. After three more calls, he proposed to Jane and Longbourn was overflowing with good wishes and celebration.

Perhaps due to all the excitement, Mr. Collins proposed to Mary. Everyone had quite forgotten he was there, for he had spent most days turning pages for Mary in the music room or researching the sermons she had recommended to him. Both seemed pleased with the engagement and Mrs. Bennet was once again full of exclamations and tears of joy. Elizabeth seriously began to wonder if her mother would have an apoplexy and encouraged Mrs. Bennet to rest, aided by some of her mulberry wine.

Mr. Collins returned to Kent, and Mrs. Bennet began planning a wedding for Mary near the new year and another for Jane three weeks later. She was determined that Jane deserved her own ceremony, far above that of Mr. Collins, and it therefore required more careful planning. Bingley would have liked to marry sooner, but he agreed with Mrs. Bennet on the benefits of a separate ceremony. He did not relish the idea of seeing Mr. Collins at the altar when he married Jane.

Soon the Gardiners arrived for the festive season and all were merry. Lydia was not happy about her new restrictions, but she could admit, only to herself and never out loud, that it was not so very bad. Truthfully, she had never realized the officers thought of her as her father said they did, and she was rather disturbed by the idea of them discussing her in such a crude manner, not to mention her abject terror at becoming with child. She was in no hurry to become a mother, no matter how handsome the officer.

Mary was wed to Mr. Collins on the twenty-ninth of December and Mrs. Bennet cried throughout the entire ceremony, then crowed throughout the entire wedding breakfast. The happy couple left for Kent after an hour spent celebrating with the family, and Mrs. Bennet waved off her middle daughter happily, secure in the knowledge that Longbourn would remain in the family for years to come.

The Gardiners returned to London in the new year and took Jane and Elizabeth with them. They would shop for Jane's wedding clothes and return for the ceremony, then Elizabeth would spend the Season in Town with them. She had seemed a bit down and Mrs. Gardiner thought the change of scenery might do her some good.

Bingley took the opportunity to go to Town himself to meet with his lawyers and prepare for his upcoming nuptials. He rode alongside the carriage and Jane watched him through the window, sighing every ten minutes. Elizabeth rolled her eyes and barely managed to keep down her breakfast.

Her aunt was right. Elizabeth was feeling low, but it was not because Jane was leaving. Netherfield was nearby and Mr. Bingley would make an excellent brother. She had no cause to repine on that count.

She was missing Mr. Darcy. He had left Netherfield with the Bingley sisters and not returned. He had not taken his leave of the neighborhood, nor sent a note to her father, nor made any effort whatsoever to contact her. It could have been easily done through Bingley. She did not require a clandestine meeting or a secret love letter. But she would have liked some sort of message. She knew he had said goodbye at Netherfield, and she had known it was forever when he said it. But at the time, forever had only been twenty-four hours and she would see him again, fresh and with no memory of the previous day. If she had known she *truly* would not see him again, she might have done something differently. She might have said more, or at least said a proper goodbye.

And her letter! How humiliating! He had likely been shocked and disgusted by her audacity. That she would write such a thing, and then go so far as to sneak into his room and leave it on his pillow! What had she been thinking? She never would have done it had she known it would last more than a few hours. He had probably burned it, maybe without even reading it—she partially hoped that was the case—or he might have laughed at it, as she feared in her darker moments. After all, he had never said anything about romantic feelings. It had only ever been tender looks and longing glances.

Had it all been in her imagination? Had she concocted this elaborate story in her mind when there was nothing there in reality? Had his kindness been only kindness and nothing more? Had all his attention been merely civility?

She would go mad with this kind of thinking. She told herself it did not matter regardless. She would likely never see him again. Even if he came for Jane's wedding—and there had been no word that he would—she would be so busy with her family they would have no opportunity to converse.

She would put him out of her mind. There was no other way.

~

London was a wonderful distraction, as were her Gardiner cousins. They kept her occupied and her mind off things she'd prefer to forget.

One afternoon, as she was sitting on the floor of the family parlor with baby Margaret, Mr. Bingley was announced. Mr. Bingley had come every day of their visit and the staff had been told to bring him to the small parlor directly. Thus, when he entered, Elizabeth had not had time to rise from the floor, nor to dislodge her young cousin from her skirts. She smiled at her almost-brother and was about to apologize for not rising to greet him when she saw a tall man walking in behind him.

"Mr. Darcy!" she squeaked.

Before she could register what was happening, Margaret started screaming for a reason nobody could fathom and Jane was apologizing to their guests for the racket. Elizabeth rose as well as she could with an eighteen-month-old in her lap and left the room with the baby, promising to return shortly.

She took Margaret up to the nursery and left her with the nurse, then made her way back downstairs. She could hear her aunt and Bingley conversing in the parlor, and not feeling up to company yet, she sank onto the stairs and let her head fall into her hands. To be caught in such an unladylike position! She was so embarrassed.

Telling herself to calm down and face the situation like a lady, she took a deep breath and raised her head only to meet the concerned gaze of Mr. Darcy.

Her mouth dropped open and she almost spoke, but she could think of nothing to say. He seemed to have a similar difficulty and they stared at each other for some time. Elizabeth finally recalled she was sitting on a step and rose to her feet.

"Miss Elizabeth, would you join me for a short stroll?"

She nodded and said she would inform her aunt. Soon, she was walking down the cold January street next to Mr. Darcy with Bingley and Jane blithely walking ahead of them.

She was desperate to know if he had read her letter, but she could not bring herself to ask.

"Miss Elizabeth," he began, "I want to apologize for leaving the neighborhood without taking proper leave of you or your family."

"It is forgiven, Mr. Darcy."

"I thank you. Miss Elizabeth," he hesitated, searching for words, and she hoped he wasn't preparing to tell her how unwelcome and inappropriate her ridiculous letter had been. She steeled herself for the blow.

"May I call on you?"

"Pardon me?" she asked, not believing her ears.

"May I call on you? Here in London? And perhaps in Hertfordshire as well?"

"You wish to call on me?"

"Yes."

"In Gracechurch Street?"

"Yes."

"You are not disgusted by me?"

"Disgusted? How could I be disgusted by you? Why would you think such a thing?"

"No reason." She would not bring up the letter if he would not.

"Then I may call?"

"Yes, you may call."

He placed his hand over hers where it rested on his arm. She told herself to calm and took deep breaths, wondering why he wasn't flustered at all. *Of course, he isn't flustered. This is Mr. Darcy!* They walked to the end of the street and into a small park in silence, somewhere between content and anxious.

It was Elizabeth who finally broke the silence. "May I ask, Mr. Darcy, what changed your mind?"

"About courting you?"

"Yes." She appreciated that he did not pretend not to know what she referred to.

"You did."

"Me?"

"Yes. I am a Darcy, the son of a rich man and connected to a powerful family. I am young, and therefore something of value on the marriage mart, much as I dislike it. Many women have tried to show me what good wives they would make, and more than one family has approached me for an alliance." He looked away with a pinched expression. "None of them were truly interested in me, but in what I could do for them, what I could give them. The status they might attain through me and the lifestyle they could have as my wife."

She squeezed his arm in support and he returned her look of sympathy with an almost smile.

"I was disgusted by it. I understand the merits of a political marriage and those entered into for social or financial advantage. I understood them very well in Hertfordshire. But I did not want to live that way. I knew I should, I knew it was my duty, but, I could not make myself do it." He was quiet again, and she waited patiently until he was ready to continue. His voice was soft when he spoke.

"My cousin, Lord Milton, was wed three years ago. Suffice it to say his marriage is not happy. He and his wife are rarely in the same house, let alone sharing a table. They have a son and a daughter and are now happy to have nothing to do with each other beyond what is strictly necessary. They see their children rarely, and each other even less." He looked at the ground and said quietly, "I want more for myself."

"I understand," she said gently.

"I do not want to forego Pemberley because I am avoiding my wife. I do not want to seek my fulfillment outside my marriage, and make a mockery of my vows, because my wife cannot stand the sight of me. That is not the way of happiness."

"No, it is not."

"Your letter—" she flinched and he gallantly pretended not to notice— "was the answer to all my wishes. It taught me to hope, as I had scarcely ever allowed myself to hope before. That you saw me as a man, as a friend, was, is, amazing to me." He turned to face her and took both her hands in his. "That you saw my attraction to you and did not even attempt to use it to your own advantage—my God, Elizabeth! Do you know how rare you are?"

She looked at him wide-eyed and open-mouthed. He placed a finger beneath her chin and gently closed her mouth. "Dearest, loveliest Elizabeth. How could I not love such a worthy woman?"

"But you left!" she cried. She cringed at her outburst, her mind in a whirl of confusion and bliss.

He flinched and stood a little straighter. "I did. I am sorry. I was more than a little conflicted, and I thought I might forget you with some distance." She couldn't hide the hurt in her eyes and he looked back at her sadly. He brought her hands to his chest and held them there tightly. "But I could not forget you, and more importantly, I did not truly want to. What folly that would have been! You are a woman worthy of being pleased, and I have learned what it means to live without you. I do not wish to do so ever again."

She gave him a wobbly smile and tried desperately not to cry. He looked back at her sweetly and stroked her cheek, and she leaned into his hand.

"I have missed you so very much," she whispered.

"I am so sorry I stayed away, my love. It will never happen again."

She nodded, her throat too tight to speak.

"Does this mean you will marry me?" he asked.

"I thought you were asking to court me."

"I was. Now I believe we are beyond that. Will you marry me, Elizabeth? I do not wish to be parted from you ever again."

"Yes! I will marry you quite happily, Mr. Darcy." She smiled brilliantly at him and he returned it with the widest smile she had ever seen from him.

He raised her hand to his lips and kissed it gently. "Call me Fitzwilliam."

~

Mr. Gardiner was quickly applied to and his permission readily given. A letter was sent to Longbourn and Mr. Bennet sent a reply a week later—quick by his standards—giving Mr. Darcy permission to marry his favorite daughter.

True to his word, Darcy refused to leave Elizabeth. Everywhere she went, he accompanied her. He introduced her to his sister, whom she immediately liked, and to his uncle the earl, whom she was immediately wary of. She met his favorite cousin, a Colonel Fitzwilliam, and she wished she had had a brother like him. He was very nearly the male embodiment of herself and she began to understand her betrothed a bit better. His great-uncle Darcy was a judge with a very dry wit. Overall, she was quite pleased with her new relations.

Darcy attained a special license and though it was quick, it was decided they would share their wedding day with Jane and Charles, only a fortnight away. Charles was thrilled to be gaining his closest friend as a brother and he and Elizabeth quickly began calling each other Charlie and Lizzy. Jane smiled at their antics, and Darcy tried to reciprocate by asking Jane to call him Fitzwilliam, but sweet Jane had seen how awkward it made him and asked if she might simply call him Darcy, as her dear Bingley did. Darcy was terribly relieved and even brought himself to call her Jane on more than one occasion.

~

Mrs. Bennet had never been happier than the day she married off her two eldest daughters in the grandest wedding Meryton had ever seen. The brides were resplendent and the breakfast was a feast fit for royalty. Darcy and Elizabeth left for London two hours into the celebration, but Mrs. Bennet was satisfied by Jane and Bingley's continued presence. Elizabeth had never been gladder Mr. Bingley had let Netherfield and not Mr. Darcy. It was possible to be settled *too* near one's family.

Two days before their wedding, as he turned pages for her at the instrument while the snow swirled wildly outside the window, Darcy asked Elizabeth what she had meant when she wrote in her letter that she thanked him for sharing so much of himself with her. And for that matter, how had she known so many things before he told her? Like Wickham's perfidy, or the story about riding with his cousin and avoiding the collapsed well. When he told it to her, she had not seemed surprised at all.

Her reply was simple. "Do you believe in premonitions, Mr. Darcy?"

Epilogue

Pemberley, Six Months Later

"Is that a letter from your cousin Anthony?" asked Elizabeth as she settled next to her husband on the sofa.

"Yes. Sarah is expecting a child in early autumn. He is beside himself with pride," said Darcy.

Elizabeth smiled and curled up next to him. "Can you blame him?"

"Of course not." He was unable to resist kissing her rosy cheek, regardless of their location in the morning room. "You know, it is strange," he added thoughtfully.

"What is strange, my dear?"

"Anthony sent me a letter while I was at Netherfield telling me how he had recently become engaged to a woman in the next parish. He was astounded at his good fortune—that he had found so worthy a woman, that she had an equal affection for him, and that they were able to marry, even though he was but a vicar."

"He is hardly a pauper! He is the son of an earl."

"True, but he believed she would have loved him regardless of who his parents were. I can admit to you now that I was terribly jealous." She looked at him in surprise and he continued, "First sons are often pursued heavily, and it is not because they are more worthy. As an only son who had already inherited, I had seen more than enough drawing room machinations."

She rested her head on his shoulder for a moment. "You poor dear! How hunted you must have felt."

He ignored her tease, as he often did. "As I sat there, reading Anthony's letter, I couldn't help wishing that I would know such love, such pure affection for myself. I wished for it most fervently," he added in a soft tone with a kiss to her hair. "But I could not think how it could happen. When would a woman ever be close enough to me, when would I allow her close enough, to learn to love me? I would have never spent such time with a woman for fear of raising her expectations."

Elizabeth raised her head from his shoulder and leaned back to look at him, her face reflecting incredulity and a dawning horror. "You wished for a woman to learn to love you?"

He touched his finger to her nose gently. "I would say my wish was answered most satisfactorily."

Elizabeth burst into laughter.

The End

Chapter 15

The Gentleman's Perspective

Darcy fell into his bed, exhausted in mind and body. The evening had been a series of small tortures. Miss Bingley's flattery, the noise and bustle of the ball, his own confusion and conflicting emotions had all combined to leave him weary and short-tempered. And he had had the strangest dreams.

He seldom had more than one in a night, but last night was very odd. He dreamt Miss Elizabeth Bennet had kissed him outside Netherfield and said goodbye with tears in her eyes. He had felt so helpless, so very sorry for her distress, and yet, when he tried to go after her, his feet would not move. He had awoken disturbed and anxious.

He continued to see strange flashes of her in his mind throughout the day. They were laughing as they danced at the ball, talking of everything from feathers to their families and childhoods. He imagined confiding in her and felt the sweet warmth of her trust and trustworthiness. His mind was so muddled he could no longer tell what had been a dream in the night and what was wishful thinking.

He had been unable to resist asking her to dance. He requested the fourth set. Not as momentous as the first or the last, and not as tempting as the supper set. He wanted to remember her laughing eyes and sweet smile long after this night. He knew it was foolhardy, that the more time he spent with her the harder it would be to leave her, but he had great faith in his self-control, and he would do as he ought. He would not be swayed from his duty by the daughter of a lowly country squire. He could enjoy the dance, watch her skirt swirling around her ankles and the curls on her neck bouncing as she danced about him. He could enjoy her company and her smiles and leave with his dignity intact. He could and he would.

But he had miscalculated the lady. She had seen through him, as if he were made of glass, and all his pretensions of leaving without encouraging her had been for naught. Her farewell in the library told him as much. She knew. She knew he was fascinated by her and she also knew he would do nothing to act on it. He would leave her, and she knew exactly why.

To his great surprise, Darcy felt a shadow of shame settle over him.

He knew he had to be realistic, that he was dealing in real life and not in fairy tales, and that as much as he might care for her, as well as he believed they would do together, he had a duty to his family and to his heritage to advance the family's holdings and status. Georgiana would make a better match if he married well. If his bride were well-dowered, he could expand his own fortune and enrich Pemberley for his heirs.

If he married Elizabeth Bennet, his lands would not be expanded, his sister would have no additional support, and the dozen children he was sure he would have with Elizabeth would have less funding from their father.

He sighed. There was no point in dwelling on what could be. He must focus on what should be. He rolled over restlessly, tired but unable to sleep, and something poked his face. He reached blindly beside his pillow and found a piece of parchment. Curious, he carried it over to the fire and looked at the seal on the back. It was plain. His name was written on the front in a hand he did not recognize.

He had thought the letter might be from Miss Bingley, but he knew her hand from the many notes she had sent him while staying at Netherfield. Her letters were much larger and looping. This was a neat, precise hand.

He lit a candle and settled into the chair by the fire, his curiosity winning over his desire to sleep. By the end of the second sentence he knew who the author was, but he darted his eyes to the end of the page to be sure. In his shock at seeing her name so boldly written, he dropped the letter. He stared at it for a moment, wondering if he should read it (and fearing for his own resolve if he did), until he could bear his mind's questions no more and took it up once again.

You have become very dear to me. Good god! He had realized that she knew of his intention to leave Netherfield and why he must do so, but for her to hold him in the same esteem! And she knew they could never be together. She saw the chasm between them as well as he did. Why had he thought they were not a fairy tale? They were a dark tale indeed—a cautionary tale.

He continued reading, shocked that he had been so transparent. He had felt the danger of paying her too much attention, but she had felt his regard nonetheless. How she saw through his feeble attempts to hide his true feelings! He felt exposed, embarrassed, and oddly relieved.

Guard your heart—protect it fiercely—as I would do if I had the privilege. He closed his eyes and breathed deeply. She wished him to protect his heart! She wished him to find contentment and true companionship. He dropped his hand to his lap and his head to the back of the chair. Oh, how he wished he could have found that contentment and companionship with her! How he wished the little dreams he had, the visions of their future, were to be a reality.

You will live long in my memory as the first gentleman of my acquaintance. Did she know he would never forget her as long as he lived? He could not understand what she meant by his trust in her. But then she had known he would not understand her words. How well she understood him!

And his affection was not unrequited! The lover in him longed to hear those words, while the practical gentleman loathed every syllable. His torture was now complete. He had touched her heart, but he would never touch her lips, nor have her hand.

He tucked the letter away in his writing desk and tried to sleep. It was no use. He could not fall asleep until the letter was safely under his pillow, grasped tightly in his fingers.

~

He would not feel guilt. He would not. He stared out the carriage window, watching Hertfordshire fade away, and tried not to think of her.

Miss Bingley attempted to convince him to speak to Charles about Jane Bennet. She knew her brother would listen to Darcy, and Darcy knew Bingley would not listen to his sisters alone. Darcy wanted the best for his friend, but in truth, he did not know the contents of Jane Bennet's heart. When Bingley asked him, Darcy told the truth. He had not paid close enough attention to Bingley's interactions with Miss Bennet to know one way or another. If Bingley was truly interested in her, he should return to Netherfield and find out for himself.

Elizabeth Bennet had not taken advantage of Darcy when it would have been easy—and to her material advantage—to do so. She had been a true friend to him. He would be likewise to her. Darcy would not speak against Elizabeth's beloved sister.

~

Three weeks. It had been three long weeks since Darcy left Hertfordshire for London. Bingley had returned and claimed Miss Bennet's hand. The letter had been full of blots and incomplete sentences, but his friend's joy leapt from the page. Darcy immediately wrote his congratulations and wished his friend joy. He did not ask about Miss Elizabeth. He would never move past her if he did not turn his mind elsewhere. It was the only way.

~

Christmas was upon them. He purchased sheet music for Georgiana and a small brooch he thought she would like. There had been a pair of emerald earrings at the jeweler's that would have looked very well on Miss Elizabeth, but he hardly thought of her when he saw them. The love song his sister played, perfectly pitched for Miss Elizabeth's high, sweet voice, barely reminded him of her. He had almost forgotten her. She had only crossed his mind four times today, not counting the dream that lingered when he woke and the tiny bout of daydreaming as he sat by the fire.

The real Miss Elizabeth would never stand on a carriage step with a stubborn gleam in her eyes. He would never kiss her hand and flirt so blatantly. And she certainly would not kiss his cheek and drive away before he could respond. He was imagining things. It did not count as thinking of her if the images were not based in reality.

She was almost forgotten, truly.

~

This dream was worse than the others. He had been so happy, so completely content. Waking up alone and cold, the fire burned low and the bed curtains drawn tight, only reinforced to him how very much he had lost—had given up. He forced his mind to empty, but in the end, only holding her letter, which he was in a fair way to knowing by heart, would help him sleep. She cared for him enough to let him go. He would follow her example.

~

Winter was such a dreary season, and it wasn't even halfway through. He trudged downstairs to the breakfast room, attempting to appear his usual fastidious self and failing miserably. The staff gave him a wide berth, though he was too distracted to notice.

He opened his correspondence at the breakfast table. Anthony had written again of his betrothed. For a vicar, his cousin was bordering on poetic. Anthony Fitzwilliam was a younger son of the Earl of Matlock. He and Darcy had grown up together and had long had a steady friendship. Anthony and his brother Richard, now a colonel in the regulars, had often spent summers with Darcy in their youth. Richard was two years Darcy's senior, and Darcy was less than a year older than Anthony. The three of them had many happy memories together.

Darcy was happy for Anthony, truly he was, but he tired of hearing of his cousin's unending joy. Miss Sarah Swanson was the daughter of a local landowner and unknown to Darcy. She came from a respectable family and possessed a dowry of twelve thousand pounds. She was moderately connected—her father was a distant cousin of the Earl of Hardwick and her mother was a first cousin to Lady Nichols, the wife of Sir Henry Nichols, a baronet with extensive property in Suffolk.

The Fitzwilliam family had approved the match. The girl was very pretty and possessed excellent manners, her dowry and connections were good enough, though not as good as they could be, and her father was the wealthiest man for twenty miles in every direction. Darcy secretly thought the Fitzwilliams approved because though Anthony was a man of the cloth, he was known to have a stubborn streak as wide as the channel. If he wanted to marry Miss Swanson, marry her he would. The family would not risk a public rift and would support him with all the appearance of joy in his choice.

Anthony waxed on for two pages on how very lovely Sarah was. How sweet, how kind, how melodious her voice and how soft her skin. Darcy was nauseated by the time he came to the end of it. Had everyone gone mad? Anthony was barely recognizable and Bingley was acting a mooncalf over Miss Bennet, but at least his letters were only marginally legible.

Darcy couldn't help the bitter huff from escaping his mouth. Anthony had been concerned over the family's reaction to his betrothed. Ha! At least she had a dowry to speak of. Her father's estate would be inherited by her brother, not a distant cousin too ridiculous to claim as a relation. She had ties to the nobility—distant, but ties nonetheless. If his Miss Bennet had possessed but one of those things, he would have paid his addresses weeks ago.

What was he thinking? She was not his Miss Bennet. She was not *his* anything at all.

~

Darcy passed another week in what he could only deem to be the most acute mental distress of his life before deciding to seek assistance. He knew exactly where to turn. As a breed, Darcys had long been known as fair, rational, thinking men. No one embodied that more than his great uncle, the judge.

Darcy was let into his uncle's house shortly after dinner and quickly invited to sit by the fire with a glass of port and a blanket for his knees. He accepted the port and declined the blanket. His uncle was glad to see him and asked after his health and his sister before fixing his nephew with a shrewd eye and asking what had brought him to see his old uncle in the cold of a January night.

Darcy could not refuse the honest request for information and offer of assistance, and soon the entire story was laid out. He spoke of his time in Hertfordshire, of his unwilling attraction to a country girl that grew stronger each time he saw her. He spoke warmly of her wit, her intelligence, her kindness and forbearance in the face of great provocation.

His uncle nodded knowingly, having met Miss Bingley on more than one occasion.

Darcy held nothing back. His uncle soon knew of Miss Bennet's letter and his conflicting feelings regarding it. The judge was told of Darcy's disturbing dreams (though not in great detail) and his concern over returning for Bingley's wedding and being unable to hide his affection for Miss Elizabeth Bennet.

"So your great question is whether or not you should attend your friend's wedding?"

"I suppose."

"You do not sound certain."

Darcy hesitated and looked around the room, anywhere to avoid his uncle's astute gaze.

"Do you believe I have done the right thing?" he finally asked, his voice so low it could barely be heard over the logs crackling in the fireplace.

"Let us look at this logically," stated the judge. He leaned back and crossed his hands over his lap, looking every inch the impartial observer. "Miss Bennet is a gentleman's daughter, is she not?"

"Yes, she is."

"Her family's estate is one of longstanding?"

"Yes, I believe she said seven generations."

"That is impressive."

"Yes," said Darcy quietly.

"She has no useful connections?"

"None that I am aware of. One maternal uncle is an attorney in Meryton, the other has a business here in Town. I know not of Mr. Bennet's family other than that he has a distant cousin named Collins who is to inherit his estate."

"Ah, yes, the entailment. That brings me to my next question. Does she have a dowry?"

"I have heard that she has roughly a thousand pounds, but I know no details."

The judge nodded. "Interesting, is it not, that were the estate not entailed away from the female line, her elder sister would be set to inherit and the family would be considerably better off? We would likely not be having this conversation."

Darcy paused to think. If Jane Bennet were in line to inherit Longbourn, would he have hesitated to connect himself to the Bennets?

"The mother, the sisters, they are wholly unsuitable," added Darcy.

"So is Lady Catherine, but she is family, so you must endure her company." The judge spoke without emotion, his expression neutral.

Darcy looked at him with some surprise.

"Come now, nephew, surely you see that Lady Catherine is allowed to continue as she does because she has rank and wealth. If you say Mrs. Bennet is a terror, I trust your judgment, but I will be hard pressed to believe she is any worse than Lady Catherine." He peered at Darcy over his spectacles and Darcy was forced to concede that Mrs. Bennet was not truly any more embarrassing than his own aunt.

"Now, we have established that Miss Bennet brings little to the table in terms of money and connections, which is lamentable, but she is not unsuitable by birth, which is in her favor. Is Pemberley in need of funds? Will you be able to weather the disbursement of Georgiana's dowry with little trouble?"

"No, the estate is not in need of funds. Georgiana's dowry will cause no lasting hardship. I could well weather a dowerless bride."

"Very well, we have established that a lack of dowry is no encumbrance. Are you in need of connections?"

"Not truly. I do not relish spending more time in Town than I already do. I would be happy to spend the majority of the year at Pemberley."

"A country girl would be more inclined to that idea than a lady of the ton."

Darcy nodded in acknowledgement.

"What of Georgiana? Would they get on?"

"I believe so. Miss Bennet is kind to her own sisters, even the ones who try her nerves more often than not. I cannot see that she would have any real trouble learning to care for Georgiana. Her liveliness would likely be a good complement to Georgiana's shyness."

"Yes, she might help little Georgie come out of her shell," he said thoughtfully. "Very well. She is suitable by birth, and her lack of dowry and connections are not a problem for you. Her temperament is likely well-suited to the family you have and the life you wish to lead. Is she healthy?"

Darcy flushed. "Yes, she appears to be."

"With five daughters so close together, her mother must be fecund," said the judge casually. "That bodes well for you. You require an heir, and Pemberley is not entailed away from the female line. Should she prove like her mother and give you only daughters, it would be no hardship, though you might regret the loss of a son."

Darcy nodded. "I might, but a son is not guaranteed in any union."

"Ah, and here we come to the material point. You could marry a well-dowered lady with laudable connections if you so choose. Why do you fixate on Miss Bennet? Have you lost your heart to her? Is that why you bother an old man with your questions?" He said the last with a teasing smile and Darcy returned it.

"I believe I have, Uncle. Would that I could change it."

"Why should you? Nephew," he leaned forward and spoke earnestly, "there is no true impediment. She may have some rough edges that need smoothing out, but your Fitzwilliam cousins would surely help you. Margaret has always doted on you and it will be years before her daughters are old enough to launch for a season. She would leap at a project of this size." He laughed softly at the thought. "You are your own man and may make your own decisions—it cannot be lack of permission that deters you. We have established that her birth is not disgraceful, though her mother and sisters will have to be kept out of the public eye. That should not be so very hard. They rarely travel to London and the younger are too young to reasonably be brought to Town for a season. You do not need money." He looked at his nephew with probing eyes. "Why do you hesitate?"

"What if I am making a foolish mistake in the heat of passion?" Darcy said quietly.

"Ah, I see. May I say, Nephew, you never do anything in the heat of passion. Would that someone could inspire you to impetuosity!"

Darcy looked up from where he had been studying the carpet to gape at his uncle.

"Fitzwilliam, allow me to tell you something. An honest woman in our sphere of society is a rare and wondrous thing. I do not mean to say that most women are *dis*honest, but they are taught from the cradle to tell a man what he wishes to hear, to subsume their opinion to his. Many men prefer this, I daresay, but I know you are not one of them. Neither am I. If I want nothing but obedience, I will get a dog." He huffed and sipped his port.

"From all you have told me, your Miss Bennet does not seem to be cowed by you. She has brought out a spark in you I have not seen since your father was alive. I thank her for that alone. But what truly impresses me about this young lady is that she knew her power over you and did nothing. Nothing! She cared only for your benefit. She could have brought you to heel had she a mind to," said the judge with a hard look and the shake of one bony finger.

Darcy looked offended and his uncle laughed at him.

"Be honest with yourself, man! You were in the palm of her hand. You still are." He ignored Darcy's injured expression and continued speaking. "When she could have had all of Pemberley and a good husband besides, she chose to let you go, with her blessing. She did not spurn you or rail at you for abandoning her." He leaned back and leveled his nephew with a stern stare. "I have seen enough in court to know that very few people will deny their own comfort and advancement for the sake of another. It is not to be taken lightly."

Darcy looked into his uncle's dark eyes, so like his own, and saw the truth of his statement. He sighed and ran his hands through his hair, still feeling fraught with indecision and torn between his heart and his duty.

"If you cannot bear the public scrutiny that comes with choosing a dowerless, unknown bride, then perhaps it is *you* who does not deserve *her*."

Darcy stared at his uncle, offended and shocked at his statement. Judge Darcy stared back, utterly unperturbed.

Finally, the judge broke the silence with softly spoken words. "Fitzwilliam, a life heavy with regret is hard to bear. Remember that."

Darcy said goodnight and made his way home, his mind full. Had they truly come to the logical conclusion that Elizabeth was a good match? She had proved her goodness and loyalty by not seeking to entrap him. She loved the country and would be a good and fair mistress of Pemberley. She was a gentleman's daughter. Where was the impediment?

~

It took Darcy two days to realize he was an idiot of the first water. Elizabeth had offered to let him go when she thought their alliance impossible and had wished him well in the future. In contrast, he had snuck off like a thief in the night, with no proper leave taking and no recognition of her kindness, no thanks for her selflessness.

Was he a coward? Afraid to face the woman he loved because… he did not know why. His reasons had gone up in smoke and blown away in the wind. His uncle was right. He did not deserve her.

~

Darcy awoke the next morning filled with resolve. This could not continue. He would seek out Miss Elizabeth and ask to court her properly. His uncle had confirmed what he had long felt to be true. A woman like that did not come along every day. He had always known she was unique—that was what had drawn him to her—but his fear that others would not see it, that his family name would be damaged by others' opinion of her and her family, and his decision to choose her, had held him back. It was cowardly and he was more than a little disgusted with himself.

Well, no more.

He saw how wrong his thinking had been. Elizabeth would not degrade the family name. She would be its greatest asset. She would be an exemplary mistress, a wonderful mother, and an excellent sister to Georgiana. He knew without a shadow of a doubt that she would be a perfect wife to him—a true wife. A lover and companion.

He felt the full weight of his stupidity for fighting it all this time. What kind of man willingly stayed away from Elizabeth Bennet? Only a fool would do something so senseless.

And Darcy was no fool. Not anymore.

Chapter 16

An Overdue Visit

Darcy sat in the carriage, nervously tapping his foot on the floor. Bingley was content to stare out the window with a ridiculous smile on his face, oblivious to the world around him.

Darcy could not be so glib. His entire future happiness rested on the result of today's interview. If she refused his request to call on her, he did not know what he would do. Would she refuse to even see him? His heart pounded at the notion. Surely, she was too generous to do such a thing. But if she planned to deny him, would it not be a kindness to refuse to admit him? His mind leapt from one unlikely outcome to another like a rabbit in a field—or Bingley in a ballroom.

Stop it! You are being ridiculous. Elizabeth will not refuse to see you.

He took a deep breath and turned his mind to other things. He had sent his Uncle Darcy a note once he had made the decision to pursue Elizabeth. His uncle had written back immediately.

Ha! I knew you would come to your senses eventually. It might have taken longer on your own, but sooner or later, you would have run into her at some party or ball or some house in the country and been unable to restrain yourself.

Go to it, man! And bring her to meet me as soon as you can. I wish to see this paragon of virtue for myself.

B. Darcy

Darcy had grinned and shaken his head at the reply. Leave it to his uncle to make the complicated seem so very simple. Darcy was sure the judge and Elizabeth would get along splendidly.

~

Darcy entered the house on Gracechurch Street with quick steps he had to modulate lest he run over the maid leading them in. He followed Bingley into a comfortable parlor at the back of the house, and there she was. Sitting on the floor of all places, with an adorable baby on her lap. She was smiling—at Bingley, not himself, but he could imagine it was for him. He was instantly flooded with the image of coming home to just such a family scene, but she would be sitting at Pemberley, not her uncle's house, and it would be their child on her lap, not her cousin. And her smile would be for him, not Bingley.

He saw the instant she realized Bingley wasn't alone. Her smile fell away and her eyes widened in shock. Perhaps he should have sent a note. Before he could think more, the baby began squalling and Elizabeth was struggling to her feet. She said something that could not be heard over the din of the baby's cries, and then she was gone.

He stared after her, wondering if she would come back.

Bingley quickly seated himself next to Miss Bennet and Darcy stepped back into the hall, hoping for some privacy and a moment to collect himself. This was not how he had imagined their first meeting would proceed. He would come to the door, she would invite him to sit. He would take the seat nearest her and they would begin to talk. Nowhere in his plans had there been a baby, or anyone sitting on the floor, and most definitely no crying and running from the room.

He heard someone hurrying down the stairs and stepped forward, hoping to meet Elizabeth. She sat on the step, her elbows on her knees and her face in her hands, looking forlorn. He wished to comfort her, but he knew not how, and he was acutely aware that he was the cause of her distress.

Finally, she looked up and he met her eyes. He tried to smile, but his face felt tight and he was unsure of his success. Eventually, she stood and he managed to ask her if she would like to walk out. She quickly gathered her things, informed her aunt, and somehow asked Jane and Bingley to join them.

They were walking down the street, Darcy feeling both thrilled by her presence on his arm and lost for words, when he decided to begin his apology. She forgave him readily, as he had hoped she would. The time was upon him. He must ask her if she would see him again. As a suitor. He swallowed thickly.

"May I call on you?" he blurted. He closed his eyes at his ineptitude, but she did not seem to notice.

"Pardon me?" she asked.

"May I call on you? Here in London? And perhaps in Hertfordshire as well?" Did his voice sound as desperate to her as it did to him?

"You wish to call on me?"

"Yes."

"In Gracechurch Street?"

"Yes."

"You are not disgusted by me?"

"Disgusted?" he cried. Wherever had she gotten such a notion? "How could I be disgusted by you? Why would you think such a thing?"

"No reason."

"Then I may call?"

"Yes, you may call."

He thought she seemed nervous, but that was to be expected. The important thing was that she had given him permission to call on her. All else would sort itself out, he was certain. He placed his hand over hers where it rested on his arm, content for the first time since he left Netherfield. He led her to the end of the street and into a small park in silence, happier than he had felt in ages.

It was Elizabeth who finally spoke. "May I ask, Mr. Darcy, what changed your mind?"

"About courting you?" He would not pretend ignorance of her meaning.

"Yes."

"You did."

"Me?"

She was so artless, so genuine. What had he been thinking when he left Netherfield?

"Yes. I am a Darcy, the son of a rich man and connected to a powerful family. I am young, and therefore something of value on the marriage mart, much as I dislike it. Many women have tried to show me what good wives they would make, and more than one family has approached me for an alliance." He looked away, feeling all the repulsion of the idea. "None of them were truly interested in me, but in what I could do for them, what I could give them. The status they might attain through me and the lifestyle they could have as my wife."

She squeezed his arm and he looked at her softly, her compassion once more brought to his attention. He sighed.

"I was disgusted by it. I understand the merits of a political marriage and those entered into for social or financial advantage. I understood them very well in Hertfordshire. But I did not want to live that way. I knew I should, I knew it was my duty, but, I could not make myself do it." His voice faded away.

"My cousin, Lord Milton, was wed three years ago. Suffice it to say his marriage is not happy. He and his wife are rarely in the same house, let alone sharing a table. They have a son and a daughter and are now happy to have nothing to do with each other beyond what is strictly necessary. They see their children rarely, and each other even less." He looked at the ground and said quietly, "I want more for myself."

"I understand," she said gently.

He looked at her with bright eyes, hoping she understood all he was trying to tell her. "I do not want to forego Pemberley because I am avoiding my wife. I do not want to seek my fulfillment outside my marriage, and make a mockery of my vows, because my wife cannot stand the sight of me. That is not the way of happiness."

"No, it is not."

"Your letter was the answer to all my wishes. It taught me to hope, as I had scarcely ever allowed myself to hope before. That you saw me as a man, as a friend, was, is, amazing to me." He turned to face her and took both her hands in his. "That you saw my attraction to you and did not even attempt to use it to your own advantage—my God, Elizabeth! Do you know how rare you are?"

She looked at him wide-eyed and open-mouthed. He placed a finger beneath her chin and gently closed her mouth, amused at her surprise. "Dearest, loveliest Elizabeth. How could I not love such a worthy woman?"

"But you left!" she cried.

He flinched and stood a little straighter. "I did. I am sorry. I was more than a little conflicted, and I thought I might forget you with some distance." He looked at her wide green eyes, filled with hurt and betrayal, and he felt all the shame of having caused her pain. He brought her hands to his chest and held them there tightly. "But I could not forget you, and more importantly, I did not truly want to. What folly that would have been! You are a woman worthy of being pleased, and I have learned what it means to live without you. I do not wish to do so ever again."

She gave him a wobbly smile and he saw tears in her eyes, but she seemed determined not to let them fall. He looked back at her, his heart in his eyes, and stroked her cheek, and she leaned into his hand.

"I have missed you so very much," she whispered.

He swallowed. She had missed him! "I am so sorry I stayed away, my love. It will never happen again."

She nodded.

"Does this mean you will marry me?" he asked. It was what he had truly wanted to ask her all along, but he had not wished to rush her. Now, they had shared so much, a courtship almost seemed a step backward.

"I thought you were asking to court me."

"I was. Now I believe we are beyond that. Will you marry me, Elizabeth? I do not wish to be parted from you ever again."

"Yes! I will marry you quite happily, Mr. Darcy." She smiled brilliantly at him and he knew his face was covered with a grin that would do Bingley justice.

He raised her hand to his lips and kissed it gently. "Call me Fitzwilliam."

The End

~~Truly~~

For Now

About the Author

Elizabeth Adams is a book-loving, tango-dancing, Austen enthusiast. She loves old houses and thinks birthdays should be celebrated with trips—as should most occasions. She can often be found by a sunny window with a cup of hot tea and a book in her hand.

She writes romantic comedy and comedic tragedy in both historic and modern settings.

You can find more information, short stories, and outtakes at EAdamswrites.com

Historical Fiction
The Houseguest
Unwilling
Meryton Vignettes
On Equal Ground
The 26th of November

Contemporary Fiction
Green Card
Ship to Shore

Printed in Great Britain
by Amazon